THE MATCH

Sam Whitelock

THE *Match*

SAM WHITELOCK

CHAMPIONSHIP ROMANCE SERIES

Book 1 – The Race

Book 2 – The Game

Book 3 – The Match

Book 4 – The Break

Copy Editing by English Proper Editing Service

ISBN: 978-82-694836-0-4
Publisher: Sam Whitelock

BLURB

LILY

My final project in college takes an unexpected turn when the athlete I was supposed to follow drops out at the last minute. Suddenly, I'm going to London and spending weeks with Sebastian, a man who's always seen me as nothing more than his best friend's little sister. This might be my chance to prove him wrong and push us past friendship into something more.

SEBASTIAN

Being the subject of Lily's project would be easy if she were anyone else. But she's my best friend's sister. The one woman I've wanted for far too long, and the one I've kept my distance from because of it. Now she's closer than ever before, and I can feel my self-control slipping every day I spend with her.

A funny, steamy football romance where the tension is high and the reward even greater.

Dedication

This one is for all those who have wondered if that fine line should be crossed.

It should.

Acknowledgements

Thank you to Larissa for once again creating the beautiful cover for this book, bringing the characters and their story to life.

Cover Artist: Larissa K. Designs
Website: larissakdesigns.squarespace.com

Thank you to Jasmine and the team at English Proper Editing Service for editing and your lovely commentary on The Match.

A huge thank you to all my BETA readers who have helped me develop this story at different stages of the writing process.

♪♫ *Playlist*

Dancing on My Own – Robyn

Heather – Conan Grey

She will be loved – Maroon 5

Fuck up The Friendship – Leah Kate

Lose Control – Teddy Swims

Club Can't Handle Me – Flo Rida Ft. David Guetta

Iris – The Goo Goo Dolls

Photograph – Ed Sheeran

A Thousand Years – Christina Perri

10,000 Hours – Dan + Shay (Feat. Justin Bieber)

Trigger warnings

Sexual content

Explicit language

Table of Contents

Chapter 1

Sebastian

I'm seated at the table, enjoying dinner with my best friend and his family, when the mistake happens.

"You could do your project on me," I say, instantly regretting the words, but also knowing there is no way back from here.

Why the hell did I do that?

Lily turns toward me with a breathtaking smile that makes my breath catch.

Christ.

I'm in so much trouble here.

And I just added to that trouble, big time.

"Really, Sebastian? That would be amazing," she says, not detecting the inner turmoil I'm currently dealing with.

No wonder she doesn't catch on. Hiding my feelings from this girl has become my specialty.

Her brother, my dear best friend, Luke, seems to appreciate the idea as well.

"Yeah, that would be great, Sebastian. And then I wouldn't have to worry about some jock going after my sister," he chuckles.

Hell.

I'm actually going to hell.

He would probably not be as pleased if he knew just how much I would do for his sister. I'm probably not much better than those jocks he talks about, but at least I would never disrespect his sister or our friendship.

That's why Lily Hastings is off limits, and she will continue to be so.

She's the sister of my best friend, and that line can never be crossed.

That's why I'm sitting here, contemplating the stroke I must have suffered when I proposed that she could do her sports psychology project on me.

There is no other reason I would volunteer for this.

This is a disaster waiting to happen.

As part of her final assignment in college, Lily is supposed to follow an athlete and gather information through interviews for her paper.

She will follow an athlete and conduct her own research into their psychology and performance. Lily was supposed to cover a female tennis athlete, but she just pulled out on her.

This leaves Lily without an athlete just two days before she was supposed to start her project.

As a pro athlete, I blurted out the suggestion before I could stop myself.

And now I must suffer the consequences of my actions.

I play professional football in Europe, more specifically in London.

Even though my fellow Americans like to call me a traitor, I am living my biggest dream over the pond.

And now I invited Lily Hastings to spend the next six weeks together with me, in London, alone.

Christ.

I need to fix this mess.

Preferably, take back my offer.

As soon as the thought occurs, I cast a look at Lily.

For the first time since we sat down for this dinner, she genuinely seems happy again.

She's always been a carefree and cheerful person, and her frustration was evident for a situation she couldn't control.

I could never turn her away. I care too much about her to hurt her.

She's someone I consider a good friend, and her defeat over the situation tore at me as I sat there, thinking I could help.

So even though it may test my restraint, I decide that I will do this for her.

I want to help her—as her friend.

Because that's what we are. And friends help each other, no big deal.

~

"All ready to head back to Europe?" Luke asks me.

I've just finished packing up my suitcase, which luckily wasn't too much bother.

Whenever I make the trip back home, I try to pack light, and seeing as Lily will be coming back with me, I'm sure she'll bring enough weight for both of us.

"Yeah, your sister will probably maximise our luggage allowance," I say, a smile breaking out at the thought.

Lily Hastings likes dressing up, and it shows.

Ever since I realised that I would be going through with this, the anticipation has been brewing.

Wondering about how this will all play out.

Lily's been bouncing around ever since I provided a solution to her problem. Seeing her joy and excitement is all the answer I need to the question if this was the right thing to do.

It might test me, but I know she appreciates it.

My phone rings, and just like the three other times this week, the number is unknown.

I know who's at the other end of the line, though.

I sigh and silence my phone before putting it back into my pocket.

Luke catches my expression, grimacing when he realises.

"She's still bothering you?"

She being a girl I was stupid enough to hook up with a few months ago.

We were out celebrating a good game result, and I was dealing with some complicated feelings about Lily.

I'd just seen her at a gala in Australia and was fully intending on acting on my feelings when Luke interrupted our moment.

When I got back to London, I tried moving on from this crush once and for all, and my first step was to hook up with someone.

It's safe to say the plan was shit.

Not only did I find the first girl who could resemble her in looks, but I found someone who clearly knew all about who I was, but pretended she didn't until it was too late.

I hooked up with her at the bar, and when she wanted to take it a step further by calling me by both my names, without me telling her, I realised she might be more of a fan than someone I could bring home.

I tried to politely turn her down, but she's been bothering me, to the line of harassment ever since.

Sometimes, it will be weeks between her trying to contact me, but then she will pop up again.

"Yeah. I might have to change my number, again. This is getting ridiculous."

Luke gives me a sympathetic look. I've changed the number twice already, but she always seems to find a way to contact me again.

"She hasn't shown up at the complex yet?"

He's referring to the apartment complex where I'm living.

Ever since the clinginess started, I decided to move to a more secure building with more safety measures, in case she decided to take it a step further.

"God no. And I really hope it stays that way."

It's not like I fear for her, but it's not a good feeling having someone try to gain your attention and affection when you've made it clear that it won't happen.

"Let me know when you get that new number, then," Luke says, chuckling.

I shake my head at the absurdity of the situation.

I just wish I had never met her, to be honest.

"I will."

Chapter 2

Lily

I'm packing up my suitcase, still contemplating the turn of events yesterday.

I can't believe Sebastian offered me to do my project on him.

Or part of me can believe it.

He looks at me like the silly little sister of his best friend, who's always followed them around like a lost puppy.

He probably pitied me, considering the situation I was put in when the athlete pulled out on me at the last minute.

And we're first and foremost, good friends.

We have been for as long as I can remember. Growing up, he and Luke were like a package deal, always up to no good.

The other small part of me—that really seems to be screaming at me whenever he's near—is hoping that maybe he also feels something more than just friendship vibes between us.

When we were younger, it was just a silly crush, which Luke would tease me about constantly, and Sebastian would shrug it off.

As we've gotten older, though, it does feel different.

Still, I'm unsure if it's my wishful thinking getting ahead of me, or actual changes between us.

There have been some instances when he's definitely given me some looks that wouldn't be classified as friendly. But he's never done anything or made a move that would suggest he'd be interested in anything more than a friendship.

I'd almost convinced myself that I had to get over this silly crush.

Then, this opportunity presented itself—or rather, Sebastian offered it up—which sends my heart racing.

"All ready for Europe?" Jessica asks me, coming into my room.

Jessica is Luke's girlfriend and my ultimate supporter in the whole "Get Sebastian's attention" project.

So far, though, we've had little luck.

She's also a good friend, always there for a phone call or girl time whenever I get to travel and visit them on the road for the Formula 1 circus.

Luke is the current leader of the F1 world championship, and if he continues at the same pace as he's done so far this season, he will be crowned world champion very soon.

And maybe even more incredible, he's met the love of his life in Jessica.

"Yeah, I can't believe I will be traveling to Europe when I was supposed to be staying in Seattle."

The plan was to stay in Seattle, where I'm attending college and where the tennis player was based, but now I will be jetting off to Europe.

"Yeah, the world works in mysterious ways, doesn't it?" Jessica asks, a knowing smile on her lips.

I roll my eyes at her.

She may not have given up our little project just yet, even if I've tried to tell her numerous times that he doesn't seem keen on making any moves.

"Jessica, you've seen for yourself, he's not interested. I should probably just let this go. Save the last of my ego," I chuckle.

It's not like Sebastian has turned me down, but part of me is afraid that he would, if I ever dared to really be brave.

"Yeah, yeah, whatever, girl. He probably has some handsome teammates, though," she says, sending me a wink.

He undoubtedly does.

Maybe I'll get over this silly crush with a British hunk.

London certainly should have plenty of them.

~

"Please, just stay out of trouble."

I roll my eyes at my brother.

He's never going to stop saying that whenever we're parting ways.

He and Jessica are dropping us off at the airport, and he uses every opportunity to remind me to stay out of trouble.

"As I always say, dear brother. I can't make promises I won't keep."

He groans in front of me, pulling me in for another hug before ruffling my hair.

I guess I'll always be his baby sister, and he'll make sure to remind me as often as he can.

"At least you'll have Sebastian to keep you in line."

What he doesn't know is that I would really prefer it if Sebastian would drag me out of that line, preferably with him.

I don't want my brother to die of a heart attack, though, so I give him my most innocent smile before moving over to Jessica.

"Don't do something I wouldn't do," she tells me, making me chuckle.

"I promise."

Giving them a final hug, we say our goodbyes and go inside the departures hall.

Sebastian grabs a hold of my two suitcases.

"I can carry those myself," I tell him, knowing they're pretty heavy.

Packing for six weeks in Europe during the fall was difficult. Sebastian told me it can be anything from summer heat to full-on storms during September and October.

Therefore, I had to pack a little bit of everything, resulting in way too many coats and shoes, which weigh a lot.

"I got it," he grumbles under his breath, rolling the luggage in front of him as we move inside the airport.

I hurry after him, his pace fast, as if we are in a rush, when in reality, we have plenty of time before our flight leaves.

"Have I done something to upset you? Or are you just extra moody today?" I ask him, feeling like I'm pushing his buttons.

Sebastian is usually quite cheerful, like me, but whenever we're alone, he's more broody, which makes me wonder.

Maybe I do annoy him, and he's regretting ever offering to help me.

I'm not one to leave anything unsaid, though, so if I've done something that irritates him, I'd prefer for him to just tell me.

"I'm just not looking forward to a long flight," he says, finally looking over at me and losing some of the tension as his eyes find mine.

He really is beautiful.

His hair is a golden-blonde mix, with light brown peeking through. Over the summer, he's gotten a nice tan and let his hair grow, making him look a little more rugged around the edges.

I freaking love this look on him.

The young boy I grew up with has definitely grown into a man.

Now, he's also sporting a backward hat, which really shouldn't be allowed this early in the morning.

He probably doesn't want to get recognised, being the superstar footballer that he is, but still.

My lady parts could do without the backward hat.

"Okay, then."

We decide to get some food in our system and buy some snacks for the flight before we find our gate.

"Do you have my ticket?" I ask him, realising that Sebastian has arranged everything for this trip.

The flights, my accommodation, transport, everything. I'm just the passenger princess on this journey, which I'll enjoy every second of.

He hands over my ticket, and when our fingers brush, it's like I've been shocked by his touch.

I quickly pull my hand back, not wanting him to see the effect he has on me.

I really need to get a hold of this attraction to him if I'm not going to make a complete fool out of myself for these next six weeks.

When I scan the ticket, I see we're flying business class. I'm not really surprised, seeing as Sebastian always does, but still. It's nice to have a pleasant ticket when being stuck on a plane for almost ten hours.

"Pulled out the big bucks for me, Sebastian? I'm honoured," I tease him, nudging his shoulder gently.

"Like hell I would fly anything other than business when the flight is ten hours. I wanted to get a private jet, but Luke talked me out of it."

There goes my brother again, ruining everything. And what a hypocrite. He always flies private himself.

"My brother really is no fun," I say, letting out a long breath and stretching out my legs on top of my suitcase.

Sebastian looks over at me, a wistful look on his face, before he recovers and mumbles something about me being nice to my brother.

Chapter 3

Sebastian

I look over to Lily, who is fast asleep in the seat next to me. I'm grateful for Luke talking me out of the whole private jet thing.

I realise that spending time alone with her will be more challenging than anticipated.

I've always managed to keep a certain distance between us, our families close by, and not really spending time together just the two of us.

Now though.

We're going to be alone together a lot.

Lily is a beautiful girl, but even more terrifying, she is a beautiful person.

She has a fun personality and spirit that always shines brightly in every room she enters.

As she's grown, she's quickly becoming a striking woman who's turning heads everywhere she goes.

And she doesn't even seem to realise it.

When we got inside the airport, several men openly checked her out, which fucking irritated me.

She was there with me, and even though we're not a couple, they don't know that.

My taking care of her luggage should be telling enough that she's with someone.

Luckily for me, Lily seemed oblivious as she bounced around and told me about the things she wanted to see in London.

She's always striking, but when her excitement is out, she's breathtaking.

I've never been closer to overstepping that line between us than I was a few months ago.

We were all attending a gala, celebrating the legends of Formula 1. I was visiting Luke on the road, which coincided with Lily's visit to him.

When she entered that ballroom, wearing a light blue satin gown my jaw nearly hit the floor.

I hadn't seen her for a while, leading up to the gala.

And then she turned up, looking gorgeous and turning the heads of every eligible bachelor in the room.

I've never been more tempted to let her know just how beautiful I thought she was.

I almost did.

But then, Luke sauntered up to us, reminding me of all the reasons why I shouldn't.

Instead, I spent the evening counting how many men Lily danced with, each one driving me madder than the last.

Eight men.

Eight fucking dances.

Even though many of them were short, I still counted them, like my own form of self-torture.

Lily seemed oblivious to the lustful gazes of the men, always humouring them with her wit.

I, on the other hand, saw how those men looked at her. It reminded me a lot about myself, whenever I know she's not watching me back—or her brother, for that matter.

Which is precisely why this will be a challenge.

I can't act on my attraction to her, knowing that if things don't work out, we'll still have to see each other here and there.

I would also hate to ruin our friendship.

We may not spend too much time alone together, but I like Lily.

She is a woman I see as a friend, which I don't have too many of.

I sigh, leaning my head back against the seat and closing my eyes.

I can do this.

I have to practice self-control.

It shouldn't be too hard, knowing I've already done that for a few years.

As long as she doesn't push that control, we should be fine.

~

When we arrive at our building I can tell Lily will probably fall victim to the jet lag. I should have booked a flight arriving in the evening so she could go straight to bed.

Now, she really should be trying to stay awake so as not fuck up her inner clock.

She will be staying in an apartment in the same building as my own.

My condo is more than big enough for her to be staying there, but that precious control I was talking about? Yeah, it could never handle having her in my apartment.

Therefore, I've secured her an apartment in the same building, so I'll be nearby and easily accessible when she needs to meet me for her project or anything else.

"You really should try to stay awake, Lily," I tell her, seeing her eyes drift close for the tenth time during the car ride from the airport.

"Shut up, Sebastian. I just need a nap."

I chuckle at her.

A nap, my ass.

That nap will turn into a full-on sleep, and then she'll struggle.

"We'll bring in our luggage, then I'm taking you out. If you jumble up your sleeping schedule on the first day here, you'll be a mess," I tell her.

She mutters something under her breath, clearly not happy about my suggestion, but I know she'll thank me later.

~

"Lily, this better be the last one, I swear," I complain.

My mission to make her stay awake quickly turned into my worst nightmare.

She's been dragging me through every store available, stating that the two suitcases she bought with her didn't hold enough and that she needs more clothes for her "London adventure" as she calls it.

When she spots a lingerie shop, I halt in my tracks.

She won't drag me inside there, will she?

I wouldn't put it past Lily, but still.

Then I would have a whole set of new problems to deal with.

"Relax, I'll save that shop for later, without you." She winks at me.

Hell.

Now all I can imagine is Lily inside the shop, trying on skimpy lingerie.

I need to get a grip here.

It must be my own tired brain. It's just a little wired on all things Lily after spending the last twenty hours alone with her.

"We should get some food," I tell her, needing to distract my thoughts.

We find an Italian restaurant, needing a good amount of carbs to fill up after a long day.

The atmosphere is laid back and quiet, which is perfect for my tired brain.

We're shown to our table, and I realise we look like a typical couple on a date, sitting across from each other in a cosy setting.

I look around, a little anxious about photographers and fans.

I don't mind if we were photographed, but I don't know how Lily would react if her face were printed on every gossip paper tomorrow.

The British media have a rather nosy gossip tradition.

"Relax, Sebastian. You look like you're going to have a stroke. Afraid we'll be photographed, and I'll ruin your Playboy reputation?" Lily teases me from across the table.

"I'm not a Playboy. I was actually thinking about you and your lack of sleep. Would you be happy with your face across all the papers tomorrow?"

Lily always looks beautiful, and this is no exception. I can tell she's tired, though.

She put her hair in a braid earlier, and bits and pieces are sticking out at all angles.

Her usual spotless makeup has gradually disappeared throughout the day.

"Are you saying I look like shit?" she asks me, raising her eyebrows.

Hell.

Why did I say anything?

Now I look like an asshole.

"Eh, no, Lily. That's not what I meant. Shit. I'm sorry, this is all coming out wrong," I say, dragging a hand through my hair.

One day with this girl and my brain is already at half its capacity.

Lily chuckles at me, which lessens my nerves a little.

"I'm just joking, Sebastian. Relax." She picks up her menu, clearly not offended by my comment.

Still, I feel bad for even implying that she didn't look picture-worthy.

"You look beautiful. You always do," I say, my voice low as I pick up my own menu.

Lily casts her eyes at me over the rim of her menu, a slight content smile on her lips, before her eyes drop down to the menu again.

The next few weeks will be hard, but something tells me they'll be amazing, too.

Chapter 4

Lily

I don't know if it's the jetlag that's messing with my brain, making me hallucinate and imagine things.

Sebastian just called me beautiful.

I can't help but smile at his compliment, and his obvious discomfort when he thought he had insulted me.

Sebastian James being flustered was something I never thought I would see.

It's been a long day, and as he suspected, I'm not too keen on being photographed by a bunch of paparazzi when we've stayed awake all day to avoid jetlag.

I can't wait to get back to my fabulous apartment, take a long shower, and wash away a tiring day, before falling into bed, preferably sleeping for at least twelve hours.

"We should make a schedule for our meetings, and I'll send you my program of practices and games," Sebastian says.

The leading proponent of my assignment is my interview with Sebastian, in which he shares his thoughts on performing.

Calling it an interview when he's such a close friend feels a little weird, but I'm hoping we can set a professional boundary so he sees me as a researcher rather than a friend in those settings.

I want to write a stellar assignment, and I hope he'll be open and share as much as possible about how his brain works in sports.

How does he think?

What's different when he has a good game compared to a bad one?

How does he handle tough periods?

Does he have any specific routines?

I'll also be observing him during practice and games. That might be the aspect I'm looking forward to the most.

Seeing Sebastian excel in a sport he's good at—the atmosphere of eager sports fans is always electrifying.

"Yeah, I'll probably tag along for most of it, but I'll stay out of your hair," I say, hoping he won't get too tired of me hanging around.

He is a professional athlete, after all, with an intentional focus on his career, and I plan to stay in the background as much as I can so he can focus on his tasks and job.

Him taking time out of that to help me with the paper is very thoughtful of him.

"Yeah, we can go over the schedule tomorrow when we've both had a good night's sleep."

Our food arrives, and we both inhale our meal, hungry after a long day with little food in our system.

We eat in comfortable silence.

Doing this project on someone you know well has its perks.

I don't really have to build a relationship with Sebastian. I already know him, and he knows me, which makes this easier.

If my original plan didn't get abandoned, I'd have to spend some time building a relationship with the athlete, but with Sebastian, that time is spared.

When we're all finished, Sebastian pays for our meal, and we get in a taxi back to our apartment complex.

It's luxurious and beautiful, and I know the amount I'm paying for the apartment is way too little, but Sebastian wouldn't budge on telling me how much it actually was.

"Just let me take care of it," he said, just like he's said with everything else regarding this project.

The apartment, the flights, my luggage, everything. I know he's rich; football players in his league are paid extreme amounts.

Still, it leaves a sour taste in my mouth that he's paying for everything, and I'm determined to come up with something to repay him.

He may not want money, but I'd like to give him something he'd appreciate in return for helping me out.

When my other athlete pulled out of the project at the last minute, I had a full-on panic for the twenty four hours leading up to the dinner, until Sebastian saved the day.

I talked to my school, but they couldn't help me as this was so last-minute.

They even told me I could be delayed in my studies if I didn't figure this out.

Like hell I will be delayed.

I'm going to finish my studies together with the rest of my class.

Over the last two-and-a-half years, I've found my small group of people who've been through the trenches with me.

Exam periods when we realise we started reading way too late.

Lectures that felt never-ending.

Classes with too many quiet students who never raise their hands.

We're studying to become people who talk to others about the ups and downs of sports. The least you'll have to do is speak to others.

Oh well.

Not my problem.

I quickly found my group consisting of my closest friend, Mira. She's the same age as me, and is off to do her project in American football.

Then we have Kait, who will test her seasickness and follow a professional sailor in Australia.

Lastly, we have Wendy, who is off to sunny Brazil to work on her project about a beach volleyball player.

We are nothing but widespread, at least.

We've decided that each Sunday will be our catch-up—at least, we'll try.

With me in Europe, Kait in Australia, and Wendy in Brazil, the time difference will be a challenge, but we'll do our best.

When we get in the elevator, I ask which floor Sebastian is on. He gives me a smirk, raising one eyebrow slightly.

I catch on and roll my eyes at him for good measure.

"Sorry, mister rich as fuck, of course you have the penthouse," I say, seeing the elevator numbers closing in on the seventh floor, which is the one I'm staying at.

"Didn't know you were capable of swearing," he says, his hands resting in his pockets.

The doors open and I look back at Sebastian.

"You have no idea just how filthy I can be."

Then I wink at him and step out.

Part of me is dying to see his expression.

Another part of me is wondering if I just made a fool of myself again.

I just couldn't help myself.

He walked right into that one.

My friends always say I'm a big flirt. I don't necessarily disagree with them, but I find it harmful and fun.

Most of the time, it just pops out. Around Sebastian, I may be a little more interested in his reactions, but still, it's all entertaining.

I've seen him around a fair share of women, and I know he can be the biggest flirt if he wants to.

He's never bought out that side of himself to me, which makes me want to push him slightly.

When he called me beautiful, he was almost flustered, worried he had offended me when suggesting I wouldn't want to be photographed.

He was freaking adorable.

But I want Sebastian to be more than adorable around me.

I want him to let loose.

I want him to look at me like he looked at me at that gala before my dear brother ruined our moment.

I may set myself up for rejection here, but it will be fun, nevertheless.

You can't take yourself too seriously, and I'm going to enjoy my London adventure to the fullest.

That includes bringing out the wilder side of Sebastian as well.

Chapter 5

Sebastian

Fuck.

Everything comes back to that word and how effortlessly Lily called me "mister rich as fuck" before telling me how filthy she can be.

I don't think I've ever heard her swear before, and then she goes ahead like it's the most natural thing in the world.

And it is.

I swear all the time; most of my friends do, too.

It never makes me halt in my tracks, at a loss for words.

This really shouldn't be a big deal.

Again, I'm certain I'm going crazy.

And it has everything to do with Lily Hastings, and how freaking filthy she can be.

If I wasn't already struggling, my brain is now filled with images of her, putting her words into action.

And this is where I need to draw the fucking line.

I don't know what I expected from Lily.

But as soon as we left US soil, it's like she's even more carefree and doesn't have a worry in the world.

I've always known her to be cheerful, but this is a whole new level.

Is she flirty and daring like this with every guy she meets?

If she is, I'm going to be hanging by a thread if, or when, she talks to men on this adventure of hers.

When the doors almost close on me, I shake my head, trying to clear my thoughts as I make my way out of the elevator and to my apartment.

Usually, I would call my best friend about women's troubles. But when the woman at hand is his sister, I'm left to deal with this alone.

~

After a good night's sleep, I feel more ready to handle Lily.

We're meeting up for a late breakfast before we head to the stadium.

I take the elevator down to her floor, Lily insisting that she would make breakfast instead of heading out to a restaurant.

I don't mind, as long as I get some nutrition into my body before practice.

I knock on her door, and Lily swings it open, a bright smile on her lips.

"Morning, Sebastian."

I take in her outfit, trying not to make my admiration too obvious. She's wearing skin-tight jeans, and when she turns around, I nearly groan out loud.

Christ.

No way the guys on my team won't already notice her beauty from her face alone.

With jeans and an ass like that, she's fucking doomed.

Or maybe that's just me.

When I get a hold of myself, I follow her into the apartment and am instantly met with a delicious smell of the food Lily is cooking for us.

Now, I do groan out loud.

"It smells amazing in here, Lily. What are you making?"

I make my way over to the stove, where she's flipping something in the pan.

"I'm making omelettes and roasted potatoes. Figured you'll need protein and carbs, and vegetables are always a good idea."

My mouth nearly waters at the food in front of me. It looks incredible; smells even better.

How Lily has managed to get all these groceries already is beyond me.

That's one of the things I forgot to think about when getting the apartment ready for her.

Luckily, the apartment was already furnished, so I didn't have to call in too many favours.

I made sure she had clean, fresh bed sheets, towels, soap, and things she probably hadn't prioritised in those two big suitcases of hers.

My own personal housekeeper and chef helped me get everything ready for her.

Now, Lily seems to have everything she needs to cook a delicious meal, together with fresh berries, juice, and fresh bread, which she's plating up as I watch her.

I'm excited for Lily to meet Harriet who works for me; an elderly woman who seemed very interested in meeting Lily when I called and asked her to help me get everything ready for her.

And her interest in my getting the apartment as prepared as possible for this "friend" of mine, as she put it, made her very curious.

Although I insisted we were just friends, Harriet wasn't convinced, saying it seemed like a lot of effort for a "friend".

When I told her that Lily is the sister of my best friend, she just shrugged her shoulders and said, "I'm just saying this is a lot of effort, Sebastian James. I like it."

Harriet is the only one who uses both of my names, even though I've told her to keep to Sebastian.

She insists on calling me James as well, saying it's more mature and that I should embrace it.

The only other person who occasionally uses my double name is my mother, and only when I'm in trouble. I've grown out of most lectures beginning with "Sebastian James Bennet."

I'm curious to see how Lily and Harriet will get along. I have a feeling the women will become quick friends.

Harriet cooks great meals all the time, but it feels different, in a good way, to have Lily preparing something for us to enjoy together.

I look through Lily's cabinets, setting the table whilst she finishes and plates the food before we sit down.

When I take the first bite my eyes roll back in my head as my taste buds go on a journey.

"That good, huh?" Lily asks me, clearly pleased with her cooking abilities.

She seemed to enjoy herself whilst cooking, humming along to the music from the speakers and moving around her new space effectively.

I'm glad to see her adapting quickly to her apartment.

"Yes, this is amazing, Lily. I might have to come down for breakfast often," I say, looking forward to seeing what she'll come up with next time.

"Great. I can cook a stellar dinner as well," she says, and after this meal, I have no doubts.

It's not just the food, but the company.

Even though I love Harriet and we often share meals, it's not the same as having a meal with a friend or family member.

When I moved to Europe to pursue my football career, it felt like a dream come true.

My athletic dreams have come true ever since I took that step, but it also comes at a cost, in some ways.

Not having my family and friends as close as I used to is the top one.

Suddenly, everyday things like having a meal with family or friends became something I missed dearly.

I've made great friends on the team, and I invite them over to my condo once a week.

Sometimes we order takeout and play video games. Other times, we'll enjoy a meal cooked by Harriet and play board games or poker.

Having breakfast with Lily is different, in a good way. It feels like a little bit of home wrapped up in a person whom I got to take with me from the US.

Even though the guys on the team are great, we're still colleagues in a way.

And although Lily and I are as well, technically—or at least working partners for her project—we're first and foremost friends.

"I'm so excited to see the stadium. Do you think I can watch the practice from the bench?"

Lily is eager to learn more about the sport, and I'm excited to teach her all about football.

It's quite different from American football, but she'll get the hang of it quickly.

"Probably not, but you can probably sit quite near, catching all the action."

She gives a thoughtful look.

"How old is your coach?"

"I don't know, maybe forty?" I say, unsure where she's going with this.

"Should be no trouble seducing him, then. I will be at that bench in no time."

I nearly choke on my food.

When I go to take a sip of my drink, it gets even worse, and I start coughing.

Lily starts laughing hysterically on the other side of the table, drying tears that are gathering in her eyes.

"Oh God, Sebastian. I'm just joking. Do you need me to do the Heimlich manoeuvre on you?"

I manage to calm down my breathing and coughing, making it easier to inhale again.

When I get a hold of myself, I take a calm breath.

"No, I'm fine," I say dryly.

I can tell Lily is struggling to hold her amusement, and when I catch her eyes, we both start laughing.

This girl is going to be the death of me, literally.

Chapter 6

Lily

When we get to the stadium, Sebastian is my personal tour guide, showing me around.

We begin with the most exciting part: the field. Seeing the massive size in real life is surreal, knowing these players run around the field for at least ninety minutes.

Could never be me.

I do enjoy exercise, but not the running kind.

I'm more of a Pilates girl lately, and I'm looking forward to checking out some studios in the city.

When we go past the benches, I wink at Sebastian, making him shake his head at me, but his amusement is evident as well as his teeth come to show when he smiles.

I do love being the reason for that smile.

After he's shown me the turf, we check out one of the office areas, and when he tells me that he's talked to his team about providing me with a workspace overlooking the field, I nearly lose my composure.

He's thought of so much, even though I sprung this on him just a few days ago. I was panicked; afraid I'd be delayed in my studies.

Now I'm standing in London, with a man who seems to have thought of everything.

I go into his arms, wrapping my arms around him. Sebastian stands as still as a statue.

"You know, when two people hug, both people usually bring their arms around each other," I say into his chest, feeling the rhythm of his heart under my cheek.

His chest is solid and warm, and his scent seeps into my senses, making me let out a small sigh.

After a few seconds, he lifts his arms and gently drapes them across my back.

"Thank you for doing this, Sebastian. I appreciate it more than you know," I tell him, and look up into his face.

He gulps, then drops his arms and murmurs, "It's nothing, Lily."

It doesn't feel like nothing to me, but he's obviously not a hugger, so I step out of his arms.

"Should we continue?" I ask, desperate to make the awkwardness go away. It was just a hug; he doesn't have to be weird about it.

Men.

They can be weird about affection sometimes.

As we make our way around the stadium, Sebastian introduces me to a bunch of courteous staff and workers.

Everyone seems to know each other, and I try my best to memorise as many names as possible.

When we get to the training facilities, we meet the first of his teammates.

There are several guys in the gym, working out whilst listening to music or talking with fellow players. A group of three guys pauses their workout when they spot Sebastian and make their way over to us.

"Lily, these are some of my teammates. Not quite as good as me, obviously, but they're okay," Sebastian says, with a playful tone.

He gestures to the man closest to me, Fredrick, who has a handsome look, with light brown hair, deep brown eyes, and a bright smile directed at me as he takes my hand and gently squeezes it, introducing himself.

"I'm Fredrick. It's a pleasure to meet you, Lily. Don't listen to Sebby here; he's full of shit."

I chuckle, enjoying his fun spirit and the freaking nickname.

I've never heard anyone refer to Sebastian by anything other than his name, and I make a mental note to tease him about it later.

Next, we have Dean, a charming Brit with a buzzcut and tattoos covering his arms and up his neck. His piercing blue eyes are stunning, and I find myself envious of his looks.

What is it with athletes and having unreal good looks?

It almost seems like a requirement to become a professional athlete that you are also suited for modelling gigs.

Lastly, I'm introduced to Ian, who seems like the quiet one in the group. With his deep red hair and reserved smile, I decide that he is probably the most responsible in the group. He's also the only other American in the group; Fredrick is from Germany, and Dean is from the UK.

The idea that a sport brings people together from all over different countries is so cool, and I ask the guys if they're part of their national teams back home as well as playing here in London.

Next year, the World Cup in football is happening, and Sebastian has mentioned talks about joining Team USA.

The tournament is taking place in South Africa, and the guys seem eager to have a shot at representing their home countries.

When we're all up to date on football and the latest happenings, it's time for us to leave.

Dean steps closer to me, a flirty smile appearing as he takes my hand in his own.

"I'm available to give you a tour of London, or anywhere else, darling, whenever you want."

I swear Sebastian grumbles under his breath before he gently grabs a hold of my elbow, pulling me away from Dean and his touch.

"There will be no tours of that kind, idiot," he says to Dean, and even though I want to tell Sebastian to calm down, I don't want to upset him anymore.

"It was a pleasure guys. I'll see you around," I say before we start walking.

It quickly turns into Sebastian dragging me behind him, grumbling under his breath.

I stop in my tracks, making him halt as well.

I cross my arms and raise my eyebrows at him when he turns to me.

"Really, Sebastian? What was all that about?" I ask, not impressed by the overprotective act.

If he's going to be like this around every guy I meet on this adventure, then we're going to have a problem.

All I want is for him to acknowledge me as more than just his best friend's sister, but it feels like he's being an overprotective older brother.

Unless it's something else.

"What? You're not going to be with any of my teammates, especially not Dean," he says.

I decide to push him a little.

"What's wrong with Dean?" I challenge.

If the idiot in front of me actually knew me, he would see I don't have any genuine interest in Dean.

Sure, he's a charming, beautiful man, but he doesn't get my heart racing like the man in front of me.

"He's not good enough for you."

I scoff at him. Such a cowardly way out.

I roll my eyes, feeling the urge to grab hold of him and shake some sense into him.

"Christ, Sebastian. I'm obviously not here to look for a husband, and if I decide to be with anyone, I don't see how that's any of your business," I say, feeling my temper rise.

I'm pissed that he thinks he can dictate who I speak to, no matter if I'm interested or not.

I'm also pissed that at the first possible interaction with men around my age, he thinks it's okay to interfere, like he has any claim on me.

He's never made a real move, so unless he gets his head out of his ass, he doesn't get to lecture me about boys.

"This feels like Luke and his every lecture about staying away from men, and honestly, Sebastian, if you're going to act like an overprotective brother, we're going to have a fucking problem."

He grinds his teeth, his jaw ticking as he looks at me.

"The last fucking thing I am to you is your brother."

Then he turns and starts walking, leaving me standing there, looking after him.

The butterflies in my stomach shouldn't be this crazy over such a small comment, but I can't help it.

Sebastian just admitted that there is something between us that had nothing to do with family feelings.

I really shouldn't exploit his jealousy, if I can call it that, but something tells me that may be my way to push this man in the right direction.

Chapter 7

Sebastian

What is wrong with me?

One look at my teammates and their interested gazes on Lily, and I'm ready to fucking snap.

I have no business telling her who she can or can't talk to.

Dean just seemed a little too interested for my liking.

He's a notorious flirt and loves to use his British charm to win over the ladies. I've never cared until he turned those eyes on Lily.

I don't even bother denying it to myself.

I got jealous.

Jealous that, unlike me, he can actually do something about his interest in her.

He can ask her out, take her on a date, kiss her, and do all the things I want to do with her.

I'm left wanting someone I can never have.

But she deserves to have that chance with someone, if that's what she wants. I shouldn't have been overprotective like that.

Lily doesn't seem to mind putting me in my place, though.

Hell, seeing her all fired up excited me. She's always so joyful and carefree, and a selfish part of me was happy to rile her up a little when I was feeling murderous on the inside.

I turn the corner, then stop in my tracks and turn around.

Lily walks right into my chest, colliding with me, not expecting me to stop so abruptly.

I steady her with my hands on her arms before I clear my throat and step back.

"I'm sorry about that, Lily. I shouldn't have acted like that," I say, not daring to promise her that it won't happen again.

I'm quickly learning that my self-control and actions around this woman are getting thinner each day.

I don't want to make promises I can't keep.

Still, I don't want to upset her, and I did act out of line.

Lily looks at me, slightly furrowing her brows before she quietly says, "No worries," before walking past me.

She almost seemed disappointed that I just apologised to her.

I stand there, confusion clouding my brain as I wonder if I'll be able to handle this woman and my complicated feelings for her over the next six weeks.

~

I'm running up and down the field, warming up before practice, when Dean hunts me down.

I can tell this isn't a conversation I'm going to enjoy from his smug expression.

"So," he says with the biggest fucking smile ever. It almost looks scary.

"So," I reply dryly.

He starts jogging beside me, and I up my pace, hoping I'll be able to drop him.

No such luck.

"Your girl, Lily. She seems fun," he says, making me exhale hard.

I knew this was coming.

He probably saw my interest in her right away.

Dean is the closest friend I have on the team, and after Luke, I would say he's one of my best friends.

We were both new to the team when we found each other and quickly realised we were pretty similar.

Part of me really wants to talk to him about my conflicting feelings about her and the whole best-friend-sister thing.

Another part of me doesn't think it will add much value, since I can't do anything about it either way.

"She's not my girl," I mutter, feeling like the moodiest bastard ever.

"Well then, it should be no problem if I ask her out," Dean says, which makes me stop.

He looks at me, raising a brow, reminding me a lot of the blonde who occupies what's left of my brain.

"You're not going to do that," I state, not too keen on explaining myself, but also knowing Dean won't back down from this.

I know I wouldn't if the roles were reversed.

"What's the deal then, Sebastian? Come on, man, I'm your best mate on this team. You can tell me," he says, hitting me lightly in the shoulder.

I don't know what to tell him, and at my silence, he comes up with his own theories.

"Let me guess. She has a boyfriend, or maybe a girlfriend?"

I shake my head at him, but he only keeps going, enjoying my misery.

Dean likes coming up with his own stories, letting his imagination run wild.

"Oh, wait, you had sex with her and couldn't get your little man to function?"

Christ, this guy. He needs to be checked in somewhere.

"Hell, Dean. Absolutely not. There is nothing wrong with my sexual abilities," I say, and he cuts in before I'm finished with my sentence.

"Just bad sex then?"

"I've never had sex with her, you idiot. I've never done anything with her. She's the sister of my best friend."

It clicks then.

Dean suddenly looks like he's solved every damn problem in the world.

Then he makes an expression that is giving pity on a whole new level.

"Shit, man, that is rough," he says, throwing his arm around me.

"No wonder you looked at her like she was your next meal. You want her to be, but can't even have a tiny taste."

I shake him off me, getting aggravated again.

He's hitting a little too close to home.

"Just shut up already. I don't want to discuss this anymore," I say, and Dean lifts his hands, playing innocent.

I take a deep breath, steadying myself.

"Okay, I'll drop it for now."

Coach blows the whistle, and I'm happy to be done with this conversation, feeling ready to blow off some much-needed steam.

~

I meet up with Lily after practice, and I'm grateful the atmosphere between us seems to be back to normal, even after my weird behaviour earlier today.

Another great thing about Lily is that she's not one to hold a grudge too hard or too long.

At least, if you apologise and try to make things right again.

"You up for dinner cooked by me today? We still haven't gone over when we're going to start with the conversations relating to my project," she says from the passenger seat of my car.

She spent quite a while in the office space today before wandering down to the stadium seats and watching parts of our practice.

"Harriet has probably made dinner already, but you can eat at my place, and we'll discuss it," I tell her, knowing Harriet usually has dinner ready by the time I get back from the stadium.

"That would be lovely."

It amazes me how effortlessly Lily fits into my life. Driving back from work with her feels like the most natural thing, but then I remind myself we're not actually going back home together.

We're simply living in the same building.

And we are having dinner together.

With my chef.

When we get to my apartment, Lily goes right over to Harriet.

"You must be Harriet! Such a pleasure to meet you." The two women share a hug, and I stand back, admiring their interaction.

They're similar in a lot of ways.

Open, warm, and headstrong women.

"I must say, it's nice having a lady around, pleasure to have you, Lily," Harriet says, smiling fondly at Lily.

"Doesn't Sebastian bring all the ladies of London back to his condo?" Lily sniggers at her, the ladies having fun on my behalf.

I don't mind.

I agree with Harriet; it is nice to have Lily around. The condo can get lonely at times.

"I've never seen Sebastian James bring any girls here, actually."

Now it's time for me to interfere.

The women don't have to discuss my whole life with me standing off to the side.

"Okay, good to see that you two get along. Now, is it time for dinner?"

Lily gives me a sinister smile, letting me know she's going to get to the bottom of this.

Harriet is telling the truth.

I've never brought anyone back to my condo, preferring to keep my address as private as possible.

Especially after Ashley started blowing up my phone.

The last thing I need is meaningless hookups coming knocking later. I already have one clinger that's not letting go just yet. It's bad enough that she calls my phone and sends messages.

Therefore, Harriet's never caught me with a girl the morning after.

We sit down to eat, and it's almost like I'm not here. The two women talk each other's ears off, and I actually learn some new things about the two.

The things I do know are that Harriet went to cooking school in Paris over thirty years ago. She met her husband while there, and after that, they travelled the world, collecting recipes and culinary experiences that she eventually turned into several books.

I have each one lined up in my bookshelf, and Harriet often brings them out whenever she cooks for us.

After many years of living out of a suitcase, they ended up in London.

I was out to dinner after just moving to London when I met Harriet and her husband.

They took pity on me, eating alone in a crowded restaurant, even though I insisted it was no problem.

"Food is meant to be experienced with others," Harriet told me, and sat herself down at my table.

The rest is history, as you say.

I developed a great relationship with both of them and offered Harriet the job if she wanted it.

She and her husband are the closest thing I have to friends here, outside of the team.

When Harriet finishes the story, Lily sighs.

"Oh, wow. That's wonderful, Harriet."

Harriet also tells Lily about her husband and how they're planning a trip this winter, but haven't decided where just yet.

I make a mental note to give her an extra-large bonus this year so they can go anywhere they want.

Next up, we talk about Lily and her degree in sports psychology.

Some of her friends are considering continuing their studies with a master's degree, but Lily hasn't decided what she wants to do just yet.

She will do whatever feels right for her, she says—the most Lily thing ever if you ask me.

Her ability to live her life to the fullest is admirable. She says she would love to gain more hands-on experience in the field, rather than spending the next two years nose-to-grindstone in more books.

If that doesn't work out, she's planning on spending some time travelling, getting a tan, and checking up on handsome men, as she says.

The notorious flirt that she is.

I imagine Lily travelling all across the world, enjoying the beach, good food, and God-forbid, checking up on the local men who're going to offer her a drink, and much more.

I stop my train of thought, hoping she'll be able to pursue the practical side of sports psychology—preferably with a women's team, where no men can derail her career.

At least, that's what I'm trying to tell myself as I sit here and observe the two women chatting away.

No matter what she decides, I know she'll excel at what she does.

Chapter 8

Lily

"I'm so full I could explode," I say, falling back onto the couch.

The dinner Harriet prepared was terrific, and I ate way too much, leaving me in the current situation where all I want to do is lie down on this couch and take a nap.

Harriet just left to go back home, so now I'm alone with Sebastian, who plops down on the sofa next to me, putting his legs up on the table.

"Should we discuss the interviews, Sebastian James? Or should I call you Sebby?" I tease him.

I can't help it.

I've met some of the people in his life today, and it was adorable hearing the nicknames they use for him. Sebastian James isn't really a nickname, since it is his name, but Harriet using both is precious.

"Knew you would bring that up."

He looks over at me with a playful glimmer in his eyes and the most breathtaking smile.

Shit. That smile is lethal for women.

Especially someone like me who's already struggling with an attraction to the man.

I get up to get my purse to distract myself from his beautiful smile and freaking dimples.

I grab my calendar and notebook.

When I'm all set, I get comfortable by tucking my legs under me.

"Okay, so I've categorised the interviews based on theme and vulnerability and have a suggestion for the order, but we'll do whatever you're comfortable with," I tell him.

"Vulnerability? What exactly are you going to ask me, Lily?"

Hopefully he won't shut me down.

For this to be beneficial for both of us, he needs to know where I'm coming from and what I expect of him. I want this assignment to be strong, and therefore, we'll have to dig deep—if he's okay with that.

"This assignment is important for me, as you know. For me to write a strong paper, I'm going to dig pretty deep into your feelings, fears, and ambitions in this sport, Sebastian. Some questions may be too personal, and you can always just tell me that you don't want to answer them," I explain, hoping he'll be open to it.

Sebastian told me he's never gone to a mental coach or therapist, which many athletes do.

Therefore, these "sessions" with me might seem very intimate.

"It's fine, Lily. I'll tell you, and if you overstep a line, I'll just put you on the first flight back to America."

He smirks at me.

"And ruin my academic career? Luke would have your ass if you ever did something to hurt me," I say, obviously joking.

Luke would probably have Sebastian's back over mine if I had asked him something too personal or made him uncomfortable.

The expression on Sebastian's face, though, looks like he would be terrified of Luke if he actually did do something to hurt me.

Gone is the playfulness that was present just mere seconds ago, and in its place is what looks like real worry.

Could it be that he's feeling this, too? But won't act on it, afraid of my brother?

Sebastian swallows.

"Yeah, he would."

Instead of dwelling on the conflicting emotions in his eyes, I clear my throat and start listing the themes I've drawn up for my assignment. All of them won't fit into the final paper, but I'd rather have too much material than too little.

For each topic, I give him a few examples of questions I'll be asking so he understands it better.

I'll ask him about his daily routines and how they change when he's heading into practice, a game, a cup, or a championship.

What are the changes?

Does he feel he needs certain things to perform at his best?

Next, I have the theme of nerves and mental toughness.

Does he get nervous?

Does he do anything to lessen the nerves?

Is he bothered by nerves, or do they work as a trigger for his concentration?

Which brings me to the following theme: focus.

What does he need to focus on?

Does it come naturally, or does he have to do something specific to get in the zone?

I also have the themes of sleep, injuries, motivation, confidence, and team dynamics.

I've tried to adjust the assignment to fit him as a football player, but since I originally planned an athlete doing individual sports, some of my questions may be a little off.

When I bring this up, Sebastian lets me know he'll let me know if the questions don't align well with a team sport.

We decide we will start with the first interview on Thursday, which is two days away.

That gives me some time to work on my questions and observe him at a few more practices before we begin.

When we're all done with the work-related stuff, I feel uncertain about what I should do.

Should I leave?

He invited me here to discuss work, and now we've done that.

I should probably leave him for the evening.

It's still quite early; the sun is just setting outside the floor-to-ceiling windows, casting a striking glow over London.

Our days here thus far have been cloudy and grey, so the beautiful sunset grabs my attention.

Just as I'm about to open my mouth and announce my departure, Sebastian beats me to it.

"Should we put on a movie?"

I relax back into the sofa, feeling those stupid butterflies flying away once again.

It's just a movie, Lily. It's not like he invited you to have a make-out session.

Now, that would be amazing.

"Yeah, sure. What do you like to watch?" I want to watch a romantic movie, or maybe an action movie, but of course, Sebastian has other ideas.

"We should watch the newest Conjuring movie, I've heard great things," he says, oblivious to my fright of horror movies.

I'd rather watch a true crime documentary—don't ask me why, events that have happened are less frightening than the ones made up in a movie.

It just is.

"Hell no, Sebastian. I don't want to watch a horror movie," I tell him, making him smirk at me.

"What? Are you afraid?" he taunts, and part of me is tempted to lie, tell him that it's not a problem.

The other part of me knows that if I agree to this, I'll probably not sleep tonight.

"Of course not."

I've lost it.

I've actually lost every brain cell available.

Why did I do that? Now I'll probably not be able to sleep tonight.

Sebastian looks at me before he hunches over for the TV remote and pulls up the movie on one of the streaming outlets.

As he clicks away at the remote, the anxiety rises in my chest.

It's just a movie; how can it be? I'm a big girl now.

I haven't watched a horror movie in ages, so maybe I've gotten over my fright.

The movie begins, and I'm cursing myself for being stupid.

Not even twenty minutes in, and I want to grab the nearest pillow and hide behind it.

The eerie music is making everything worse. I try to imagine a different song in my head, as the one in the movie is clearly chosen for dramatic effect.

When I can't take it anymore, I stand up, proclaiming I'm making popcorn—anything not to watch that dreadful movie, which will steal all of my sleep.

I look through the cabinets, searching for popcorn to pop in his microwave.

I might have spotted a package in the first cabinet I looked in, but I roam around, taking my time, so I miss the most I can of the movie.

"Bo!"

Hands come down on my shoulders, and I scream, feeling my heart racing after the fear inflicted by the movie multiply as Sebastian scares me.

He is right behind me, and he topples over in laughter when he sees my dramatic reaction to his little stunt.

"It's not funny," I grumble as I cross my arms—like a child, I know.

I may be acting childish, but so is he!

He just sneaked up on me and scared me when he obviously knew I was afraid.

"You should have just told me that you were scared, Lily," he says when he calms down his laughing.

"I wasn't scared. I just didn't want to watch a horror movie," I say, still feeling defensive.

I guess part of me still feels like a little girl in some ways, but I know many adults don't enjoy horror movies.

"Lily, your breathing was going like you were out for a run. Your hands were almost shaking in your lap, and you bit your lip continuously. Don't lie to me."

Suddenly, I'm feeling very hot.

His attention to my reactions shouldn't be a big deal; he was probably having fun at the expense of my fear, but the tingle in the nape of my neck appears nevertheless.

Who knew Sebastian picked up on so much?

"Did you even watch the movie, or just me?" I ask, not knowing what to expect of his answer, but holding my breath nonetheless.

"Mostly you, it was more entertaining," he chuckles, making my own amusement rise.

He fucking loves seeing me suffer.

And I got stubborn.

I probably should have just admitted I was scared.

"Asshole," I mutter, my own smile breaking through.

Sebastian finds the popcorn, puts it in the microwave, and gestures towards the living room.

"Come on, you can choose the movie."

We settle into the couch again, this time with me browsing through the selections.

I decide it's only fair that I get my payback by choosing the cheesiest romantic comedy I know and like.

I don't dare try anything new; I just want to watch a comfort movie after the horror of The Conjuring.

How to Lose a Guy in 10 days starts playing, and Sebastian gets up to grab the popcorn and a can of Coke Zero for me.

As a health freak, his beverage of choice is sparkling water with pomegranate flavour. His whole fridge is stocked with it.

The can of Coke Zero for me must have been something left by one of his friends, because I haven't ever since this man drink soda.

"God, you really need to start living, Sebastian," I tell him.

A can of soda won't kill him, and it's even without sugar!

"I'm living just fine, Lily."

He takes a long sip of his drink.

"I don't believe that. You probably only ever drink that or regular water. Do you go out? Have sex with girls?"

He coughs, making me laugh once again, because this is the second time today I'm making this man choke.

Some of his precious sparkling water spills on the floor whilst Sebastian struggles to calm his breathing, the carbonic acid probably making it more difficult.

"Oh, dear. I swear I'm not trying to kill you," I say, getting a flashback to this morning when I told him I'd seduce his coach to get the best seats at the stadium.

"You really need to stop talking about sex when I have food or drinks in my mouth," he mumbles, finally recovering from his coughs.

I study him, trying to read his expression but coming up pretty blank.

It's fun getting to know him better.

"Okay. I'll just talk about sex when you're not eating and drinking then."

I go back to watching the movie, feeling his eyes on me out of the peripheral of my vision.

Those damn tingles won't calm down when I feel his attention on me, but it's a pleasant feeling.

When I look over, he quickly averts his eyes, back to the TV.

Maybe I shouldn't talk about sex around this man at all. But it's so fun to see him all flustered whenever I surprise him.

I also think he does need to live a little.

Ever since we got to London, he's all work and no play. It's clear that life over here is focused on work for him, but he does live here.

That means he also needs to implement some fun in his life. I want to bring out all sides of him, and I know he's got it in himself.

He took Luke skydiving to cheer him up during a rough patch with Jessica.

I almost can't believe an adrenaline junkie like that doesn't want to enjoy a can of soda.

But the rush of a skydive or a bungee jump gives him more than soda.

It does make sense.

I pull one of the blankets over my legs and snuggle more into the sofa, enjoying the story of two people falling in love by annoying the living shit out of each other.

Chapter 9

Sebastian

I look over to Lily, finding her fast asleep beside me, still with around twenty minutes remaining of the movie.

I noticed her freaking quoting the actors earlier, so I know she loves this movie and has probably seen it more times than I can count.

It isn't the worst movie I've seen. The banter between the characters reminded me of the dynamic I've fallen into with Lily.

Growing up together, I've always known her as a fun spirit, always teasing her brother and me about various things.

And we were teasing her right back, which is why she's so quick with her retorts.

Being here alone with her makes it even more amusing.

And sizzling.

Now it's just the two of us—no one here to set those boundaries that I probably should.

I take in the sleeping beauty on my sofa. Her hair is sprawled out across the pillows behind her, and she's breathing heavy.

The urge to run my fingers down her cheek is screaming at me, but I resist—for now, at least—and continue looking at her.

For me, this is home, at least one of my homes.

Lily just packed up her life and followed me to London, when she was supposed to be staying in Seattle.

And she doesn't seem scared or anxious about anything.

Other than horror movies.

She wasn't joking when she told me I need to live a little. Her outlook on life sure seems like a lot of fun, and even though I know I can be a lot like her in that regard, I realise I may have fallen into a routine characterised by health and performance.

Which is a good thing, but I still need balance.

I decide that whilst Lily is here, I'll try to enjoy London more, knowing she'll probably drag me around to see all the sights and explore the city.

As I gaze down at her, I can't stop the urge to touch her and run my fingers lightly down her cheek.

When she stirs, but only snuggles more closely to my hand, I hold my breath, afraid she'll wake up—and really hoping she doesn't—so I can touch her a little longer.

When the movie ends, the urge to lift her into my arms and carry her to my bed so she can sleep more comfortably overwhelms me.

Restraint holds me back, knowing nothing good would come out of that.

Instead, I run my fingers down her cheek one last time before I gently shake her shoulder.

"Lily, wake up," I murmur, making her stir under me.

She wakes up, her beautiful eyes sleepy as I back out of her space.

Lily stretches her arms before she pushes herself upright on the sofa.

"I can't believe I fell asleep. That is like my favourite movie."

I stretch my legs, feeling the soreness from practice earlier today.

I may have been pushing myself a little too hard after a few days off, and now I'm feeling the ache.

"You're probably still a little jetlagged."

Lily stands up and gathers the empty bowl, my glass, and her soda can before venturing into the kitchen. I follow her—not wanting her to leave, but knowing it's inevitable.

I wonder what it would be like to have her in one of the guestrooms, but I stop my train of thought.

There is a reason she got her own apartment.

Mostly for my own good and to refrain from crossing that line.

And she deserves to have her own space, not being crowded by me every second of every day.

She goes to the door, and I stand back, gripping the counter hard to distract my hands from doing something stupid, like reaching for her.

"This was fun, and Harriet is wonderful, so I'm definitely coming back up here."

She's right, this has been fun; and of course, Harriet is the best.

The two women will probably meet up without me, considering their fast friendship.

Having Lily in my apartment felt good.

Comfortable and natural.

"Yeah, I'd like that."

With one last lingering look, she grabs the door and says goodnight before she's gone.

I'm left standing, looking at the door for way too long before I eventually get ready for bed.

~

Over the next few days, we fall into our own little routine.

I do my usual morning routine: shower, open the blinds in my apartment, and drink my ice-cold glass of water.

I get ready for the day, packing my bag for the arena and the day ahead, but instead of making my own breakfast like I usually do, I take the elevator down to Lily's apartment.

Each morning, I'm greeted by the stunning blonde, listening to music and cooking away at the stove.

I always volunteer to help and she declines every time, serving me a perfect cup of coffee before going back to cooking, whilst I watch her from the kitchen table.

Each day she's wearing a new stylish outfit, matching perfectly to the weather outside, which is rather grey and dull, but Lily doesn't seem to mind. Always eager for the day ahead and the plans she has.

It's clear that Lily pays attention to nutrition when she cooks, and even though I know she's healthy, I get the feeling she's doing the little extra for me as well, knowing I'll appreciate it.

How she manages to also make it this delicious is beyond me. My usual tame porridge is quickly becoming my least favourite breakfast, even though that's been my go-to for a long time.

Her meals are simply better in every way.

When we're all done with breakfast, I'll clean up the kitchen as she packs up her stuff before we drive together to the arena.

When we get there, we say our goodbyes for the day, with me fighting the urge to do something stupid like kiss her cheek or grab her hand.

Every day, the impulse grows stronger, but I restrain myself.

I'll do my workouts and look for her in the stands whenever we're out on the field. Dean will tease me about my obsession with her, but I don't find it in me to be bothered by it.

I know I'm in trouble with this woman, but the least I can do is look for her.

When the workday is done, we'll meet up, go back to my apartment, and enjoy dinner together with Harriet.

Then we'll finish off the evening with a movie or playing board games before Lily heads down to her apartment for the night.

On Thursday, we meet up for our interview at midday, and as expected, Lily comes prepared.

We begin with nerves and mental toughness, and I quickly realise I've never really thought much about it, but I can see how it would be beneficial to do so.

Lily is bright and to the point, prompting me to reflect on aspects of my performance I have never considered before.

Usually, I don't get nervous unless it's a game that determines qualification or a championship, where it feels like everything is on the line during those ninety minutes.

Those games energise me, pushing my teammates and me to go the extra mile and give our all on the field.

During the more regular games, I don't get the same adrenaline rush, but it's always a thrill to walk onto the field, hear the crowd's cheers, and experience the atmosphere of thousands of eager football fans.

Which is why I'm confused when I walk out into the stadium, full of nerves I don't usually experience.

My whole body is buzzing with excitement, but there's no denying the nerves there as well.

I do this several times a week, at home or away, and I've never felt this level of nerves in a regular game.

Then I remember something special about today's game.

It's the first game since coming back to London, with Lily in the stands, watching every minute.

A stupid part of my brain wants to seek her out in the crowd, but I know that's an impossible task.

I've had family and friends come and support me—mainly my older brother—Joseph, but it's been a while since someone was here cheering for me.

Harriet and her husband sometimes tag along as well.

Having Lily here sends a rush of anticipation through my body, and I'm determined to do my part to give her the best entertainment a football game can provide.

Chapter 10

Lily

It's halfway through the game, and I decide to explore the shops and look for some souvenirs to kill some time while I wait for the next period.

Sebastian's team leads 1-0, and watching them play has been exhilarating.

European football is very different from American football, yet I find myself enjoying it a lot.

The game is easy to follow, with few complicated rules. Each team has eleven players out on the field, and they're trying to put the ball in the net, simple as that.

There are some rules about offside and corners, which I'm still getting the hang of, thanks to the wonderful couple I sit beside, who explained everything whenever I asked.

I head to Sebastian's team's merchandise shop.

I want to buy his jersey and surprise him when we meet up later. The price tag makes me gawk, but I decide that this is the least I can do when Sebastian is basically paying for my whole stay.

Hopefully, he will appreciate it.

I bring the jersey over to the counter to pay, and the guy behind the stand gives me a nod of approval.

"Good choice, choosing Bennet," he says.

"Yeah, is he any good?" I ask, wanting to hear from someone who probably knows a lot more about this team and sport than I do.

"One of the best."

Hearing others praising him for his game makes me proud.

Sebastian plays midfield, which I've learned from the excellent football expert couple, and watching him run and handle the ball is majestic.

The skill, precision, and speed with which he moves are impressive. The coordination between the players and the passes works like a smooth machine, with Sebastian in the centre of it all.

I pay for the jersey and find a restroom to change into it before making my way back to my seat in time for the second period.

I'm delighted to see the couple from earlier back in their seats as well. It's nice having someone to talk to.

"Got yourself a jersey?" Craig asks me, gesturing to my new attire.

"Yes, wanted to buy myself a souvenir," I say, not quite knowing how much to reveal about my relation to the player's jersey I'm rocking.

To me, Sebastian has always just been Sebastian.

Not a celebrity.

Not a famous footballer.

All of that came after I got to know him.

The same goes for my brother. The famous Formula 1 driver chasing his first championship title.

All the fame and the celebrity status came later.

Even though I'm not the one in the public eye, I've seen how challenging it can be.

Some people change when they learn of their fame.

Which is why I keep it to myself that I know Sebastian.

Craig and Monique seem like great people, but they don't really need to know about my relationship with Sebastian.

"Bennet is great. You chose a good one!" Monique says, and we talk some more about the upcoming games.

They tell me they have a yearly membership, and both are huge football fans. Therefore, they attend most of the home games.

Sebastian's team scores one more goal before the final whistle is called. I say goodbye to Craig and Monique before heading to my new office.

Sebastian told me to go ahead and take a taxi home after the game since he'll be stuck with the media, a team recap, and a shower.

I told him I wanted to wait; this is my project after all.

I'm also excited to see his reaction to my new jersey.

I'm writing up a few ideas for my next interviews with Sebastian when he texts me that he's all ready to go and to meet him at the players' exit.

He's made sure I have an access card that allows me to enter most of the stadium.

I make my way through the halls and run into Dean and Ian. As soon as I'm close enough, I give them both a hug, congratulating them on their game.

"You did so well! It was amazing watching you guys."

"Thanks, darling," Dean drawls, looking at my jersey with a playful smile.

"Sebastian got you that?" Ian asks, and now that would be amazing.

"No, I got it from your shop. Wanted to surprise him," I tell them, and they nod their approval.

I wonder if they have any friends or family watching their games. Being a professional athlete is quite a different life from the one most people live. It's their dream come true, but it seems rather lonely at times as well, living in this football bubble whilst everyone else is off doing something different in their home countries.

"We'll see you around, Lily."

"Yes! Have a good night."

I continue down the halls and when I get to the exit, I spot Sebastian right away.

I'm bouncing over to him and throwing my arms around his neck before I can stop myself.

I'm a hugger, and he'll have to get used to that.

"You were amazing, Sebastian! I'm officially a football fan," I say, before stepping back.

Sebastian always looks good, but now? He's remarkable.

His hair is still wet from the shower, and he's wearing all black from head to toe.

The worst of all?

A freaking backward hat.

This man and his backward hats will be the death of me.

It should be illegal to look this good.

"Thanks, Lily. I'm glad you had fun."

I peel off my jacket before turning around and pointing my thumbs to his name on my back.

"What do you think?" I ask, feeling giddy from excitement.

The look on Sebastian's face, on the other hand, stops me in my tracks.

Shit.

He looks shocked.

He's staring at me, taking in the jersey, and making me feel more uncertain for each second ticking by without him saying anything.

Is this too much?

"Shit, I'm sorry. This might be a little too much. I'm—"

Chapter 11

Sebastian

I stand there, frozen by the sight in front of me.

She bought my jersey.

My team jersey.

With my name across her back.

And she looks perfect.

"Shit, I'm sorry. This might be a little too much. I'm—" I stop her before she can finish that sentence.

"No. It's perfect, Lily. You're perfect. I was just surprised," I tell her honestly.

I was already on a high after a good game. Seeing her remove her jacket to reveal my freaking jersey under it might be my favourite moment with her yet.

She lets out a breath, and a beautiful smile takes over her whole face.

"Okay, then. Good. You looked like you'd seen a ghost, so you had me worried there for a second. Everyone told me I made a good choice choosing the player."

Christ.

The need to kiss her has never been this strong.

The last few days with her have been amazing. Having Lily around is like having a ray of sunshine, even in cloudy London.

And seeing her with my name across her back, so freaking cute and proud, makes me want to march right over to her and kiss her senseless.

I can't do that, though.

"Who's everyone?" I ask, trying to distract myself from the longing burning inside me.

"Craig, Monique, and the guy at the store."

We start walking towards the parking lot, whilst Lily tells me all about her new football friends, as she calls them.

I'm glad to see her make some new friends; she's a social person, so I'm sure she'll tire of me eventually and will want to find someone else to spend her time with.

She's also learned the basics of football, and I curse myself for not explaining more to her before the game. I should have done that and given her my jersey so she wouldn't have had to spend her own money on it.

I got plenty of them.

But it was a wonderful surprise.

Game day is always hectic, so I didn't get to spend much time with her today, and I didn't use the few minutes we had together to explain football rules.

She doesn't seem to mind, and she took matters into her own hands, asking the people beside her.

I told her she could watch the game from one of the VIP boxes, but Lily insisted on staying in a regular seat.

No wonder she wanted to do that.

It would be harder to socialise with hardcore football fans from a VIP box full of celebrities, wives, and kids.

No, she'd rather be together with the rest of the fans, cheering us on whilst wearing the team merchandise.

When we get back to the apartment building and enter the elevator, I'm struck by the same feeling I've had all week.

Not wanting the night to end.

Even though my body is tired from a long day, I want to spend more time with her.

When she yawns as the elevator nears her floor, I realise she might be tired herself. The clock is nearing eleven in the evening, so it's probably wise to go to bed.

"It was amazing watching you tonight, Sebastian! I can't wait for the next game."

This is the part I always struggle with.

How to say goodbye to her.

I want to wrap her in my arms, hug her tight, kiss her cheek, her mouth, whatever she would let me.

But I can't.

Leaving me questioning how to say goodnight to her. She solves all my problems, as she does best.

Whenever I feel uncertain, she'll let me out of my misery by deciding for me.

She wraps her arms around my neck, and this time, I don't hesitate to bring my arms around her back.

Can't have her questioning my hugging abilities again.

"Good night, Sebastian," she whispers.

I give her a little squeeze to the waist.

"Good night, Lily."

Then, she steps back and out of the elevator, with me contemplating if she feels the shift between us for each minute we spend together, the same way I do.

~

I've just woken up when my phone rings. I don't even glance at the caller ID, expecting it to be one of my teammates.

"Hey, man," Luke says on the other end. Travelling all across the globe with F1 means we call each other at all different times of the day.

"Hey, man. Which continent are you on right now?" I ask, stretching my arms across my head.

"Just got to Saudi Arabia."

Luke enjoys travelling, especially after he met Jessica, as they get to experience the sights together.

My best friend is getting closer to being crowned the new F1 world champion with each passing race, and he'll hopefully have his moment in Las Vegas a few weeks from now.

I make a mental note to check my calendar and see if I can travel to Las Vegas to support him.

It's not every day your best friend can become the F1 world champion for the first time in his career.

I'm sure Lily would love to come along as well, with Luke being her brother and all.

It's like Luke has telepathic abilities, if the next question out of his mouth is proof.

"And how is my sister? Driving you insane yet?"

He has no idea.

She is driving me insane, but it has everything to do with my attraction to her and her spirit.

It may be insanity, but it feels like the best kind, even though it tests my restraints like nothing before.

"Nah, we're having a good time," I tell him, feeling my heart pound in my chest.

God, why does she have to be his sister? Everything would be so much easier if she weren't.

I don't want to raise any suspicion from Luke, but keeping my tone casual has never quite felt like such a challenge as it is in this moment.

"Making sure she's not picked up by any teammates or Brits?" Luke asks, a small chuckle escaping him.

I almost tell him that Lily is twenty-two years old and would probably get with anyone she'd like without me ever finding out.

She's always had her ways of doing exactly what she wants and making it happen.

"Yeah, but I doubt I really could stop her if she wanted to," I tell him honestly.

The whole "stay away from my teammates" speech wasn't exactly a success.

"True. Ah, I almost forgot! Congratulations on your game yesterday, it was great." I'm grateful when he changes the subject, and we start talking about all things sport.

I almost tell him that Lily bought my shirt, but I haven't fully processed it yet, so I decide against it.

It's also something that feels rather intimate—at least to me.

When we hang up, I hop in the shower before I make my way down to Lily's apartment.

Bag thrown over my shoulder, I knock on her door, and she swings it open, before she rushes straight back to the stove, probably not wanting to burn any of the food she is cooking.

I take off my shoes before I take her in.

Lily is oblivious to my stare as she cooks away and starts talking about the cathedral she wants to visit, which, according to the site she was reading, has the best view of London.

She's wearing a dark red leather skirt, paired with high boots that reach up to her knees. Black stockings cover her exposed skin from her knees to the hem of her skirt. To top it off, she has a tight black sweater and gold hoops in her ears.

Has she always dressed like this?

I realise I don't actually know how Lily dresses. It's not like I've seen her every day in the last few years.

The times I've seen her, she's looked gorgeous, just like now.

If she's going to dress like this, my attraction to her will only grow, but that seems to be the case either way, so I may be doomed no matter what.

"I'm planning on visiting the church after work, so I'll probably not eat with you and Harriet today."

I'm setting the table, and Lily brushes my side when she puts the frying pan on the table.

Just as quickly, she's gone.

The brief contact leaves me buzzing, wondering whether she did it on purpose and feels the same rush as I do from a slight touch.

"We could do it together. I can give Harriet the day off, and we'll make dinner ourselves?" I suggest as we sit down at the table, facing each other.

Considering my attraction to this woman, I should not insist on spending every available minute with her.

At the same time, we have a great time together, and I want to experience the city with her.

And I made a promise to myself to bring more fun into my life, and doing things with Lily seems to be the perfect way.

“That would be great, Sebastian. It’s a date.”

As soon as the words leave her mouth, she looks up to the ceiling and brings a hand to her forehead.

“Oh God. That’s not what I meant. I always say I have dates with my girlfriends, and I just meant it’s a deal.”

I chuckle because she’s usually the one making me say stupid shit.

It’s nice having her a little flustered as well.

“It’s fine, Lily. Don’t worry.”

Chapter 12

Lily

Luckily, Sebastian doesn't tease me too much about my mishap with having a date.

He doesn't really comment on it, which I'm grateful for, but also a little bummed.

A silly part of me was hoping he would say that we could call it a date, but the realistic part of my brain knows that's not going to happen.

At least not yet.

Before coming to London, I've felt like my attraction to the man has been one-sided.

Now? I'm not sure.

Something is definitely changing between us.

More times than one, I've seen him look at me, and dare I say, with desire in his eyes.

The squeeze to my waist when saying goodnight yesterday almost sent me into a frenzy.

I've never really been someone who craves a man's touch or attention. I like flirting, making men sweat a little before I decide whether I'm interested for real.

With Sebastian, I'm eager for even a small glance or touch. That small squeeze kept me energetic until I fell asleep.

And him calling me perfect in his jersey? I almost fell to the ground right then and there.

Whenever he suggests spending more time together, like he just did, my excitement shoots through the roof.

It could be because he pities me for doing things alone and treats me like his "guest," but he knows I have no problem taking care of myself which is why I get the feeling that he's enjoying our time together just as much as I am.

When we're done eating, Sebastian tidies up, and I pack my bag.

I could get used to this routine.

It would be even better waking up together, but for now, I'll take what I can get.

~

After a few hours of work, I head down to the stands to watch the practice.

Even though the observational part of my project won't amount to much in the final paper, I enjoy watching them play and making notes.

It's nice sitting outside for a while as well and not huddled up in an office all day. I look up at the sky, grateful to have my umbrella nearby as there is a slight drizzle in the air. Even though the English weather is quite grey, the cold hasn't set in just yet.

They practice various drills while wearing vests, then are divided into smaller groups. Dean and Sebastian play opposite each other, and when Sebastian dribbles past easily, I sigh.

He's magnificent to watch.

When Sebastian passes the ball to another player, Dean catches up to him and ruffles his hair.

They mess around a little, making me smile.

It's good to see their friendship. The whole team seems to get along well, but it's clear that Sebastian has his own group in Dean, Ian, and Fredrick.

When they're all done, Dean comes running over to where I'm seated, with Sebastian hot on his heel.

"Lily! What a delight to see you here, darling."

The British accent makes everything sound flirty. I'm sure he pulls all the ladies using that accent and his charm.

"Have a good practice?" I ask.

To me, everything looked great, but I'm still a newbie to this sport.

Sebastian catches up to us, and what a sight he is.

His hair sticks to his forehead, and when he lifts his bottle to take a long sip of his drink, the jersey lifts, revealing part of his abs underneath.

I quickly avert my eyes, but when I look into his eyes, he winks at me, a small smile evident behind his bottle.

Freaking winks at me!

He's definitely feeling the same changes as I am.

"Yes, it was good. Will you come to our game on Saturday? And game night at Sebastian's on Sunday?"

I look questionably at Sebastian.

I'm planning on attending their football match on Saturday, but as far as game night goes, this is the first I've heard of it.

Dean drops an arm around my shoulders, pulling me into his side.

"You're one of us now—that means game nights," he says, with the biggest smile towards Sebastian.

He looks at the arm draped across my shoulders before he swallows.

"I haven't talked to her about it yet, but I was planning to. You're more than welcome to come, Lily, but I also understand if you don't want to hang around a group of grabby football players."

At his tone, Dean drops his arms, rolling his eyes at his teammate.

I shouldn't be enjoying this, but I can't help myself.

Sebastian did not like Dean having his arm around me, and the grabby hands comment proves my point.

"I'd love to! I'll catch up with you when you're ready, Sebastian," I say, breaking the tension.

I grab my bag, and Sebastian drags Dean with him towards the exit of the field.

My excitement about my not-date with Sebastian this evening has just intensified.

~

"Come on. Aren't you supposed to have great stamina?" I ask Sebastian, who's moving at a pace that is nowhere near acceptable for an elite athlete.

We're moving up the stairs of St. Paul's Cathedral, and I'm eager to get to the top and see the view as the sun sets over London.

Sebastian, on the other hand, is moving like we have all the time in the world.

"There is nothing wrong with my stamina. I'm just not the biggest fan of stairs after I've been working out for four hours today."

Why did I even bring up the word stamina?

Now, all I can think about is the man behind me and his freaking stamina.

And not the kind related to walking up stairs.

I stay silent as we finally climb the last part. When I find a spot overlooking the city, I stand there in awe.

There is just something about the twinkling lights of a city that is getting ready for the evening, one light at a time.

"Wow, this is beautiful," I say, watching the colours of the sky turning pink and orange.

The clouds have mostly cleared for the day, leaving a beautiful sunset in their wake.

"Yeah, it is," Sebastian murmurs beside me.

After a little while gazing at the view, I pull out my phone and snap a few photos and videos to send to my family later.

Our group chat is quickly being filled with pictures of my adventures here, and Mom is always sending back hugs and kisses. Dad is more of a thumbs-up guy.

"Come on, get in frame, Sebby," I say, turning my phone around and having the city view behind me.

"Don't call me that, Lily," he grumbles beside me, coming closer to me, making my body light up.

"Sorry, Sebastian James," I snicker.

Sebastian quickly pinches my waist, making me jump and let out a small yelp.

This man and his touches to my waist will send me into cardiac arrest soon.

He steps up close to me, leaning down to whisper in my ear.

"Just Sebastian."

Hell. When did it get so hot out here?

Every hair on my ears, down to my toes, raises at his closeness. He smells divine, and I'm tempted to turn my head. I would probably be inclined just to kiss him right here.

But I don't dare.

"Lily, picture," he says, shaking me out of my desires.

"Yeah, right."

I bring up my phone in front of us, feeling my hands shake, and praying that he's not able to see it.

I don't turn into a quivering mess around men.

Right now, though, I'm struggling.

But this isn't just any man; this is Sebastian.

I snap a few pictures, probably smiling like a lunatic as my head is all over the place and my facial expressions are probably messed up.

All I can focus on is the man beside me and the way he's making me feel.

I really need to gain some control if I'm going to get through this evening.

Chapter 13

Sebastian

I feel my control slipping.

Day by day, minute by minute, in her presence, and I'm ready to snap.

It doesn't help the case that whenever I step closer to that line, Lily meets me halfway.

She doesn't back down or retreat from my touch.

She leans into it, making that control slither even faster.

Not even two weeks in, and the thought of kissing her is slowly driving me insane.

How am I going to survive four more weeks without overstepping that line?

I think back to my best friend, her brother.

Would he be mad?

Would he kill me?

It's not like I have a sister of my own to compare this situation to.

And it's not like I want to just sleep with her.

Of course, I want to do that as well.

But it's more than that.

I want these moments where we're experiencing something new together. Her teasing of my stamina as we climb the stairs, or a mountain, whatever she wants to do.

The shared meals with Harriet and our comfortable morning routine. Our movie nights in front of the TV.

I want those moments elevated.

Holding her hand, kissing her senseless whenever I feel like it. Cuddle with her on the sofa whilst we watch one of her romantic comedies, or when we decide on a documentary—which is our common ground.

That's what I want.

Would Luke approve of that?

I want to talk to him, but I'm freaking terrified of what it would mean for our friendship.

If it's a hard no, our friendship would be tainted, possibly ruined. And I would be devastated.

He's my best friend.

Therefore, I step back, creating more distance between us, even if it fucking crushes me when I catch the disappointment in Lily's eyes.

She quickly recovers, giving me her brilliant smile, even though I get the feeling we're both feeling the heaviness of our situation.

~

We decide to make burgers that combine all the nutrients I need, Lily tells me. She may be the passenger in this Bugatti, but whenever we're in the kitchen, she's in charge.

As I gaze over to her in the car, I'm tempted to explain my sudden shutdown, but I don't know what to say.

I'm sorry I can't kiss you and do what we both want, if your reactions are anything to go by. I'm just terrified of what it would mean for my friendship with your brother.

She deserves better than this.

I need to keep my distance from now on, even if it feels like agony.

Once again, I'm struck by Lily's ability to keep the vibes between us as usual.

Whilst I'm pondering away in my own head, she's her normal talkative self, not a hint of awkwardness.

When we get to my apartment, she starts prepping the burgers straight away, giving me strict orders to stay out of the kitchen.

"Can't have the football star nipping a finger on a knife or crying from cutting onions," she snickers.

Cooking seems to be something she enjoys, given the amount of time she's already spent preparing delicious meals for us after we arrived almost two weeks ago.

"I feel bad that you're doing everything. Put me to work, Lily," I tell her, feeling like a freaking guest in my own apartment, not being of any use.

"No, you sit your ass down and relax. You've fixed everything for me over here: volunteering to be my athlete, the apartment, the flights, and everything else. Please let me do this, Sebastian."

I sigh but do as she tells me.

If she thinks she's some burden to me, she couldn't be more wrong.

I love having her around—she feels like a piece of home just got transported to London.

We talk about the game on Saturday, which is away. Unfortunately, she can't travel with my team as she's not officially a part of the club.

It's only about forty minutes by car, so I tell her she can either drive my car, and we'll travel back together, or I'll pay for a driver.

"You'll let me drive your car? The Bugatti?"

She seems tempted by the idea.

After dwelling on it for quite some time, I decided to just buy the car. It may be a lot of money, but I can afford it.

Luke had been giving me too much shit about not having my own sportscar.

I was hesitant as I don't know how long I'll be in London for. My contract is for multiple years, but in football, anything can happen.

"Yes, but I will be driving back," I tell her.

"Hell, I can't, Sebastian. They drive on the other side of the road here. I'll probably get myself killed."

Shit, that's true.

I've gotten used to driving on the other side of the road, and switching whenever I go back home.

That's not the case for Lily.

"Driver it is."

We sit down to eat, and the first bite into the burger makes me groan out loud, which causes Lily to laugh.

The meat is the perfect amount of juicy, without being undercooked, and the vegetables bring just the right amount of flavour.

"If the whole sports psychology thing doesn't work out, I'll just hire you to make food, then you can gossip with Harriet the whole day and feed me."

The two women have become quick friends, and they share a love of cooking. The other day, Lily went home before me, and I found the two chatting away in the kitchen when I got back.

"Or we could just get married. Then you wouldn't have to pay for me to cook for you."

Lily has a teasing tone, but her words stop my movements.

I know she's just joking, and marriage isn't something I envision for myself quite yet, but the image of her in my apartment—more permanently—has crossed my mind, too many times to count ever since she got here.

"What kind of ring would you want?" I say, meeting her with the same teasing tone.

I'm also a little curious to know the answer. Lily enjoys good jewellery; she's wearing rings and a gold necklace every day.

"Not giving you the answer to that one, Bennet. That is reserved for my true future husband," she says, and the words "you're looking at him" are at the tip of my tongue.

Wow. Getting ahead of yourself here, Bennet?

What happened to keeping the distance between us?

My self-control around her is close to zero.

Our flirtatious personalities get us into these situations. We both like to flirt, and it usually doesn't mean too much.

But with our tension and connection, every interaction is sizzling.

We're tiptoeing that fine line between friendship and something more, and the flirting is definitely blurring that line.

I steer our conversation to safer ground, talking about the game night I host for some of my teammates most weekends if our schedule isn't too crazy.

Most nights, it's me, Dean, Ian, and Fredrick, but sometimes, other guys will join as well.

I was planning on inviting her, so Dean beating me to it earlier today pissed me off.

His hands all across her didn't sit well with me either. The fucker likes to mess with me now that he knows Lily is off limits to me. He uses every opportunity to do so, but I'm not worried.

I didn't miss her checking out my abs when my shirt lifted.

Her attention was all on me, even if he had his arm around her.

When the kitchen is spotless again, the clock is nearing ten, meaning there will be no movie night tonight.

I shouldn't be feeling this level of disappointment over that, but I am.

Our movie nights are always fun, and for each one, I find myself a little closer to her on that couch.

I follow Lily to the door, and like every night, I'm contemplating how to say goodnight to her, and she's solving the issue like it's not a big deal.

It probably isn't, to her.

Maybe I'm the only one going insane here.

She gives me a quick kiss to the cheek, so fast I almost miss it before she goes out the door with a "Goodnight, Sebastian" thrown my way.

That small touch of her lips leaves me energetic as I stand here, my hand on my cheek, as if I'm checking if this just happened or if it's my own imagination playing tricks on me.

Those lines I've been thinking about look a lot more like waves with no clear direction or boundaries.

Chapter 14

Lily

When I go inside my apartment, I lean against the door, letting out a breath.

What a wonderful and confusing day.

There is no doubt in my mind anymore that Sebastian is feeling this just as much as I am.

But where I want to push and move forward, I sense his hesitation.

And I can't really blame him for it either.

I know he's worried about my brother, even though he hasn't told me so himself; it's clear every time his name comes up.

He gets this clouded expression and goes into deep thought.

Therefore, I'm left to flirting, subtle touches, and the hope of Sebastian losing that precious self-control, preferably before I board the plane back to America.

I've decided he must be the one to take the first real step.

Luke will always love me; I'm his sister.

Sebastian probably feels like he could be sacrificing his friendship with Luke if he crosses the line with me.

I honestly don't know how my brother would react.

He's been teasing me from our youth about crushing on his best friend, but it's always been this harmless joke.

This doesn't feel like a joke anymore. It feels like so much more.

I'm nervous thinking about his reaction if anything were to happen between us, and I'm sure it's even worse for Sebastian.

Meaning, he's going to need to be the one who takes the final step.

I will be pushing him, though, just like I did when I gave him a small goodnight kiss.

I didn't dare to stay and linger to catch his reaction, running out the door as quickly as I could.

My phone rings, and I smile when I see it's Mira. We haven't been able to talk much since I got here.

"Hi, girl. How is sunny Texas?" Mira is working on a project about an American football player who plays in Houston, Texas.

"Hi, Lily! It's good—a lot warmer than Seattle, which is nice. How is London?"

Warmer weather does seem nice, but I've quickly grown used to the gloomy weather of London.

"It's so good. Cloudy most days, and some rain, but I don't mind."

The jetlag has finally been beaten, and my internal clock is all synched up.

We talk about our projects and how they're progressing. Even though our data collection runs for six weeks, we'll have six more weeks to complete our paper. Then we'll have our graduation, and our studies will be done.

I'm no closer to knowing what I'll be doing once that ends, but I try not to worry too much about it.

What I do know is that I want more hands-on experience in this field, as the project with Sebastian already is fuelling me so much more than reading about the dynamics in a book.

Hearing from an athlete about how he experiences stress, nerves, routine, and the various aspects has been informative.

Finally, I'm able to hear more about this from the practical side.

When our data collection ends, we'll have a few classes and meetings with our supervisors, but we've talked about booking a trip somewhere warm where we can write while getting a nice tan.

Wendy is already enjoying herself down in Brazil, so we might make our way there—or somewhere else tropical.

"Met any hot men?" I ask her, knowing Mira is almost as much of a flirt as I am.

I wouldn't be surprised if he had some manly action down in Texas. Maybe not with anyone on the team, as that could get messy, but maybe with a handsome cowboy or bull rider.

"The whole team is a beautiful bunch of men, Lily." She sighs, making me laugh.

Sounds about right.

"What about you? Any progress with the infamous Sebastian?"

I might have told Mira about my crush on Sebastian. That was before I knew I was going to travel here and have him part of my project.

"Well, yes and no. There are sparks between us, but I can tell he's hesitant—probably afraid of Luke," I tell her.

"He'll break in no time. Just bring out those sexy outfits of yours, and he'll be down to his knees in no time," she chuckles.

Mira knows I like a good outfit. One that combines sophisticated and sexy. The weather in London is the perfect fit for my wardrobe.

I felt his stare this morning when he saw my leather skirt, stockings, and boots. I might have had my back to him, but I know when I'm being watched. Before his shutdown in the church, I caught him looking several times.

"Yeah, hopefully."

~

The next day, Sebastian goes to the stadium early in the morning, as they have a full day of press, practice, and meetings.

Therefore, I'm all alone when I eat breakfast, so I decide to keep it simple with some cereal and fruit.

It's more fun cooking for two.

I feel pathetic when I actually miss Sebastian.

I can manage breakfast by myself. I've been having breakfast alone ever since I moved out.

I just saw him like ten hours ago.

When Luke calls, I smile, putting my phone in front of me as I answer his FaceTime call.

At least I can pretend to be having breakfast with him.

"There is my favourite sister," he says.

"I'm your only sister."

"Exactly."

I roll my eyes at him, the smartass. Jessica also sits down beside him, making me even more delighted.

"Hi Jessica!" I beam, and now Luke is the one rolling his eyes, muttering about his girlfriend and sister being closer to each other than him.

Jessica gives him a sloppy kiss on the cheek.

"Ah, don't be such a baby. We love you as well."

I exhale.

They make such a beautiful couple.

I'm so happy that my brother found someone like her. It also gave me a bonus-sister I'm very grateful for.

I tell them about seeing the arena and experiencing the excitement on gameday. I can't wait to do it all over again soon.

Maybe I'll make myself some more football friends as well. Talking with Monique and Craig was great.

Luke's been to several of Sebastian's games over the years, trying to support each other when their schedules align.

In two weeks, Luke can become the F1 world champion during the race weekend in Las Vegas.

I want to make the trip and be there to experience a very special moment in his career.

Hopefully, Sebastian can go as well, and we'll travel together. I know it would mean a lot to my brother to have his best friend there.

When breakfast is done and the kitchen is clean, I hang up with Jessica and Luke.

As Sebastian will be busy most of the day, I have decided to stay home and work on my paper from here.

Then I can also check out a new café for lunch, which I've been eager to visit.

I'm deep in my reading when my phone pings.

Sebastian: Not coming to the stadium today?

I smile.

So he's noticed I'm not there.

Did he look for me?

Even on a day when I know he's busy.

That's partly why I decided to stay home as well.

I don't want to burden him—make him feel like he has to babysit me and make sure I'm okay.

Lily: You stalking me?

Sebastian: Maybe.

So vague.

Now, I feel like I could die from my curiosity.

I get up, decide that I'll find that café and buy a coffee and something sweet.

Considering Sebastian doesn't eat much sugar or dessert, I must make the most of the opportunities I have.

Lily: Decided to work from home since you're busy all day.

Sebastian: Dinner tonight, then?

The butterflies in my stomach go crazy.

It's just dinner, like we have every night—with Harriet, most days.

I can't help myself when I type out my response.

Lily: It's a date. ;)

I lock up the apartment before I search for the café on my phone. It should only be about a ten minute walk.

When I get to the building lobby, a girl is talking with the receptionist. I'm studying the menu when I hear her mention Sebastian.

"Can't you just tell me which floor Sebastian is on? I promise I know him."

I decide to sit down in one of the chairs, my curiosity getting the best of me. I'm always down for a good look-out and some gossip.

I grab a magazine out of my purse, pretending I'm not spying on this exchange.

Who is this girl?

She seems to be around my age, maybe a few years older, with blonde hair; the same length as mine, actually.

A pointy nose and high cheekbones grace her face, and her makeup is on the heavier side.

The bright pink, skin-tight dress she is wearing looks more like something I would wear to a club than on a regular day, but who am I to judge?

I love myself a good outfit, and she seems to be dressing up for something—or rather someone.

She could be referring to a different Sebastian, but the chances are slim.

The receptionist looks sceptical and asks for her name.

"Ashley."

I nearly snort.

Of course her name is Ashley.

The receptionist clicks away at the computer, as Ashley stands there, impatiently clicking her heel on the floor.

Sebastian's never mentioned an Ashley, which I guess isn't that weird.

It's not like we spend our time discussing exes.

Is she an ex?

I'm certain he's not with anyone right now; then he would never be flirting this much with me. That simply goes against his character and how he is.

I regard her from my seat, wondering if this is his usual type.

"I'm sorry, miss. But there is no Ashley on the register for visitors of this building."

He's doing his job perfectly. Not revealing that Sebastian does, in fact, live in this building, which seems to be the purpose of this mission of hers.

To find him.

I'm tempted to walk up to her and do some digging myself, but I don't want to risk Sebastian and his privacy, so I stay rooted in my seat.

She huffs and puffs towards the receptionist, who only gives her an apologetic look before telling her that since she's not a resident or on any visitors list, she will have to leave.

With determined steps, she makes her way outside the door, her anger evident as her heels click loudly on the marble floor.

When she's gone, I put the magazine back in my purse before I stand up and make my way over to the spot Ashley just left.

"Hello, Miss Hastings. Is there anything I can do for you?"

"Hi! No, I was just wondering if this woman has turned up here before?"

The receptionist knows me and has seen me countless times as I arrive and leave the building with Sebastian.

He exhales, a troubled expression crossing his face.

"She's not been able to get inside the building until today, but she's been lurking around in the area for some time now. Our doorman was taking a small break, and she slipped in. I'll notify Mr. Bennet."

Christ.

Is she a stalker?

She seemed determined that she knew Sebastian, but hell, that's probably what any stalker would say.

If she's an obsessive ex, she could probably just call him to get a hold of him, right?

Turning up at his building seems rather extreme.

"Okay. Thank you for taking care of him and his privacy," I say before I head for the café.

When I get there, I order to-go, wanting to sit in the park across the street. The café is quiet, and as I wait for my order to be ready, I chew on my bottom lip, thinking back to the scene in the lobby.

What an absurd situation.

Something that started as me thinking I'd just witness a clingy ex quickly turned into something that seems a bit more serious.

Hopefully, Sebastian is all safe and will be able to deal with this.

When my name is called, I grab my coffee and cookie before I find myself a bench located under a grove of trees. The crisp autumn air leaves a fresh feeling in my lungs.

The leaves on the trees are turning darker, and I can't wait for the next few weeks when they'll be all different colours of brown, yellow, and orange.

Autumn is my favourite time of year. The perfect time to stay inside, cuddle up with a warm drink, and watch cosy movies.

I also love taking walks, feeling my cheeks turn cold as I breathe in the fresh air.

I sip my coffee, watching people walk by with their dogs, partners, and friends.

It's crazy that I'm in London—and enjoying every minute of it. As it all happened so fast, I didn't know what to expect of my time here.

How I would adapt and feel on a whole new continent and in a city I've never been to before.

For each day, I feel like I'm falling a little bit more in love: both with the city and the man who brought me here.

I sigh, thinking about Sebastian and that boundary between us.

My dear brother.

The reason I've met the man is also the hindrance between us at the moment.

Eventually, I head back to the apartment and work for a few hours.

When the clock strikes five, there is a knock on my door.

I open the door to Sebastian standing on the other side.

"Your stalking led you here?" I ask him, feeling the happiness spread through my body. My word choice makes that pit in my stomach appear again, thinking back to earlier today.

I wonder if the receptionist has told him about Ashley.

"Yes. Harriet is almost done with dinner. Come up with me?"

I notice his bag is on his shoulder, which means he came straight here from the stadium, and my heart gallops in my chest.

Did he miss me today?

I would feel a little less pathetic if he did.

I quickly grab my phone and put on some shoes before locking up.

"Speaking of stalking," I begin, feeling a bit nervous to bring this up.

What if she's someone he is hooking up with, and he simply forgot to tell the receptionist to have her name on his list of guests?

Then I'll look rather stupid, but I honestly don't care. If she's a crazy stalker, I worry about his safety.

"Did you speak with the receptionist when you got back?" I ask him as he steps into the elevator.

Sebastian looks questioningly at me.

That's a no.

"No, it was rather hectic down there. I think someone is throwing a party," he says.

I twist my hands, the nerves gnawing at me.

It's very possible I'm setting myself up for humiliation right now, but I have no choice.

"Okay. I was heading out earlier to a café, and there was a woman talking to the receptionist, asking for you."

Sebastian's eyes widen, which adds to the gut feeling that Ashley isn't someone he wants to have in his life.

"Said her name was Ashley."

"Fucking hell."

Sebastian drags a hand through his hair and paces a few steps inside the small elevator.

He stops right in front of me and brings both of his arms to my forearms, rubbing up and down.

I don't know if he's trying to calm himself down or me.

"Are you okay? Did she say anything to you?"

I can't help but smile, thinking back to my little spy operation.

I felt like one of those actors in movies, hiding behind a newspaper whilst spying on an enemy.

"Oh, she didn't say anything to me. I sat myself down and spied on her. My curiosity got the best of me."

I'm not ashamed to admit I might have a little unhealthy obsession with this man.

If he had a lady friend I didn't know about, I was planning to find out.

Sebastian lets out a breath, his hands still resting on my own as the elevator doors open.

"Okay, good. She's someone I kissed a few months back, and she's kind of been harassing me ever since. Blowing up my phone mostly, but she's never turned up here before."

Even though it doesn't feel good hearing about him with other women, it's not like we're together.

Of course, he's been with other people, just like I have.

I don't envy him and his stalker, though.

"Must have been one hell of a kiss," I say, my tone light as I gently nudge him.

Sebastian looks down at me, almost remorseful.

"Actually, I was trying to forget about you in that blue dress at the gala in Australia."

Oh, fucking hell.

Is this really happening?

Our moment at that gala has replayed more times than I can count over the last five months.

I'd chosen that blue dress for him.

Everything was for him that night.

Hoping he would finally make a move.

Which looked like he was going to until my brother showed up and ruined it.

We've both stopped in the hallway, looking at each other.

"What about the gala?" I whisper, my pulse hammering so hard I can feel it in my ears.

"You looked magnificent, Lily. I was going to tell you, but Luke interrupted us."

Magnificent.

Christ, this man and his words.

He's called me beautiful, and perfect, and now this.

If he keeps this up, I'll be doomed sooner rather than later.

Maybe I already am.

"And did it work? Trying to forget about the gala?"

I'm afraid to ask, but the memory of Ashley is still fresh in my mind.

If he's moved on, I need to know.

"Not one bit."

I stand there, lost for words—which never happens to me—but he's just given me a glimpse into his feelings, and it feels like the greatest gift.

But then, it's like watching a wall come back up.

Sebastian steps away from me, creating distance between us, crushing me as I realise he's pulling away after such a tender moment.

"I'm sorry, Lily. I probably shouldn't have told you that. My friendship with Luke is important to me, and I don't want to risk that."

Well, shit.

So much for all the words about perfect and magnificent.

He just made it clear where he stands.

My brother and his relationship with him are more important than the connection to me.

Although I do understand where he's coming from, it still stings.

We were finally making some progress, only for him to turn right back around and retreat from me.

At least I know that my attraction to him isn't one-sided.

That feels like a small consolation in the big scheme of this attraction.

Chapter 15

Sebastian

I've never had problems with saying the right thing to women, but with the one who's currently speaking with Harriet whilst we enjoy our dinner, I seem to say the wrong things most of the time.

Or I'll say the right thing, but my timing will be shit.

I don't regret telling her about how I felt about seeing her at the gala. And my lame attempt at moving past it by kissing Ashley.

What I do regret is how I handled it afterward.

Shutting down once again and basically telling her that her brother is more important to me than her.

Which isn't the case, but the hurt on her face as the words registered was like a gut-punch.

Then I have the Ashley problem on top of it all.

I can't believe she turned up here.

That's a whole new level of obsession, and frankly, I'm worried.

Not about myself, but about the beauty chatting away with my chef.

If Ashley could find out where I'm living, I'm sure she can find out that I'm connected to Lily.

The tabloids have probably posted pictures of me coming or going from this complex, and that's how she's found it.

It's only a matter of time before I'm photographed together with Lily, and she'll maybe seek her out.

After we're done with dinner, I head down to the receptionist.

He tells me the same thing Lily did: that she turned up this morning and asked which apartment I was living in, claiming to know me.

They've seen her lurking around for some weeks, but she only managed to get inside today.

Next time I decide to try to get over Lily Hastings, I need to make sure it's not with someone like Ashley.

It feels like a bad case of karma, as I deep down know I stand no chance against the woman I really want.

~

On Saturday, I'm standing in my apartment contemplating whether this is a good idea.

I have our away-game jersey in my hands, ready to be given to Lily.

Our regular one is red, but this one is white.

I figured since we're having an away game today, that it would be a good gift for her. And seeing my name across her back feels like a gift to me.

This isn't a big deal. It's just a gift.

To a friend. Who feels like a lot more than a friend, but still.

I bring the jersey with me before I can talk myself out of it, then make my way down to her apartment.

My foot bounces nervously on the floor of the elevator as it descends.

When she opens the door, she looks at the jersey in my hand, and the happiness radiates off her, and all my doubts about this gift are wiped away.

"This is for you," I tell her, handing it over.

Lily takes it and holds it up in front of her before turning it around, reading Bennet on the back, just like the one she bought herself.

"It's perfect. Thank you, Sebastian."

She goes into the bathroom, and when she emerges in the new shirt, I'm just as speechless as last time.

She looks flawless.

And mine.

She does a turn before she comes over to me. When she links her hands around my neck, I'm almost hoping she'll lean up on her toes and kiss me.

Seeing her like this is heightening my need to kiss her. I would devour her if she pressed those perfect lips to mine.

But instead, she hugs me tightly.

I soak in her touch, enjoying how perfectly her body fits mine.

When she lifts her head from my chest but doesn't step away from me, I'm not even thinking when I start closing the distance between us.

I need to taste her.

Just when my lips are nearing hers, my phone rings, ruining the moment.

I curse under my breath as I bring out my mobile.

Lily steps out of my arms and looks down at the caller ID.

Luke Hastings.

She huffs before she turns away, clearly frustrated by the interruption of her brother.

I'm hit with a wave of shame as I take the call, knowing I was just centimetres away from kissing Luke's sister—knowing I haven't come clean to him about my feelings for her.

I really should be going about this differently, but I don't have a clue how.

"Hey, man," I greet him, dragging a hand through my hair.

Hell.

What would have happened if he hadn't called at that exact time?

Would I still be kissing Lily?

Making out with her pressed to the wall?

"Hey, man! Just calling to wish you good luck tonight."

As he always does, being the best friend that he is.

His timing could use some work, though.

I'm equally frustrated and conflicted as I talk with him, knowing I was mere centimetres away from crossing that line.

A line I've vowed not to cross too many times already, and I'm feeling like that promise already is broken, knowing how I feel about her.

When I end the call, I call out to Lily, wanting to say something—anything—to her before I leave.

"I'm sorry about that. I have to leave now, but I'll see you later?" I say, unsure how to act.

The moment is definitely ruined.

Gone is the sizzling tension, and in its place is an imaginary wall where her brother's name is painted all over it.

Lily still seems upset by her brother, and my doubts have started creeping back in now that my arms aren't holding her or smelling her intoxicating perfume.

"Yeah. I'll see you later."

~

I don't get to see her later.

Our game is a total shit show, with crazy fans throwing things onto the field, interrupting the game several times as they must get rid of everything.

We're playing a match against one of our traditional arch-rivals. These games tend to get ugly, especially in the stands.

I'm worried about Lily, hoping she's seated in an area where she's safe. I always insist she stay in the VIP boxes away from the craziness. But she, of course, wants the authentic football experience.

On days like this, I feel nervous, hoping she'll be fine when I meet her later.

The madness reaches new heights when our team goes up into a two-goal lead, and I'm counting down the minutes until the final whistle blows.

The boos and the sound from the stands are loud in my ears, and I shake my head.

Just a few more minutes.

I need to get to Lily.

Due to increased security measures, we've been told we must travel back together as a team to ensure our safety. I'm not boarding that bus until I've seen Lily.

I send her a text and exhale when the three small dots start typing right away.

That's a good sign.

Lily: I'm fine! It was crazy experiencing a game like that! What an adventure!

Of course she would look at this as one of her many adventures. Everything is an adventure to her.

I ask her where she's located and make my way over to that part of the stands.

Fans are calling my name, and I sign autographs for those reaching out over the barricades.

I finally spot Lily; she's gone down to the fence, still a few metres above me, but she looks as beautiful as she did before the game.

All snuggled up with her jacket and my jersey peeking out under.

"You alright?" I ask, and people around us start calling my name.

I smile politely at them, trying not to seem like an arrogant prick, but wishing I was alone with Lily.

I had to make sure she was okay.

She rolls her eyes at me, probably thinking I'm way too dramatic.

I've seen how aggressive these games and some fans can be, sometimes leading to people being expelled who go way too far.

"Yes, go to your team. We'll meet up tomorrow. It will get late before you get back."

I'm hesitant to leave her, but I also know I don't have much choice.

She's fully capable of taking care of herself as well.

I know that—she knows that.

Still, I'd like to take care of her when I can.

Right now, though, I'm expected elsewhere.

I'm gaining attention from the people around us, so I do as Lily tells me, content with seeing her in one piece and in good spirits.

~

As the team bus nears the stadium, I get a text from Lily, letting me know she made it home safely.

"Crossed that line yet, Bennet?" Dean asks over my shoulder, looking at my text from Lily.

What a nosy bastard.

"No," I mutter, typing out my response to her and hoping he'll shut up.

No such luck.

"You could just talk to her brother. Maybe he'd understand."

Dean shrugs beside me, and he makes it sound so easy.

Luke is a great guy, and I honestly don't think he'd actually do anything to hurt me.

This is his sister, though.

That line, which Dean is asking about, is fading for each day I spend in her presence.

If Luke hadn't called earlier, I would have kissed her. No doubt.

And then what?

I'm still no closer to a solution to my problem.

"I don't know. What if he flips out, and I end up losing my best friend?"

"First of all, rude. I thought I was your best friend. Secondly, you don't know that, and yeah, it may be a risk of him flipping out, but if you plan on going down that road with her, then it's just a matter of time," he says.

That's the question.

Am I planning to go down that road with her?

I know every fibre of my body wants to.

On the other hand, Lily is a really good friend, and over these last few weeks I've had a blast with her.

What if we don't work out as a couple and I end up losing her altogether?

That would be even worse than her brother punching me for wanting his sister.

My phone vibrates, letting me know someone is calling me.

Hoping it's Lily, I look at the caller ID and groan when I see the now-familiar unknown number.

Ashley.

It must be.

I can't believe she turned up at the complex.

That means she's more persistent than I imagined.

You would have thought she would have given up by now, seeing as I've never answered any of her calls or texts.

I've thought about answering, to ask her to please leave me alone.

Like I did the first time she called me.

But that just made everything worse.

So I thought ignoring her would help.

Her turning up at my apartment complex is a whole new level of scary.

I've talked to the building owner and let them know I would prefer extra security installed.

I'll pay whatever they need.

It's not just about my safety, but Lily's as well.

I'm happy she didn't approach Ashley.

God knows what would happen then.

All I know is that I need to make sure she doesn't get to me or anyone else I care about.

Chapter 16

Lily

I stretch my arms over my head, my head filled with a dream where Luke didn't interrupt our moment yesterday.

Sebastian was going to kiss me.

He was going to take that step.

Then my brother ruined it.

The phone ringing was annoying, but when it was Luke's name flashing across the screen, I could sense Sebastian's walls coming right up again.

We were finally making some progress, but in that moment, I felt like we were back to square one.

Part of me is tempted to march up to his apartment and just kiss him.

Get it over with.

Hopefully, he would kiss me back.

The promise I made to myself, though, won't stand for that.

He must be the one to make that decision. He's the one struggling with this.

I know what I want, and don't necessarily care that much about what Luke has to say about it.

That is different for Sebastian.

I know he struggles with his loyalty to my brother, as he told me himself.

Therefore, I stay in my apartment, getting ready to make our usual breakfast, when a text from Sebastian pops up.

Sebastian: Won't be able to make it to breakfast this morning! I'll see you later for game night.

I feel like I've been punched in the stomach.

What a fucking coward he is.

Now he won't even dare be in my presence alone?

If I was uncertain about those walls before, I have my confirmation now.

I let out a frustrated huff.

I need to blow off some steam. Just as I'm ready to take a walk, my phone rings with an incoming group call from my friends.

Sunday.

Our catch-up is today.

This is just what I need: a call with my girls.

I decide I'll talk to them while I do my walk, needing to move at least to release some of the strain.

"Hi girls!" I greet them.

It's nighttime for Mira and Wendy. Kait is in Australia, so it's nearing evening there.

We take turns talking about our progress on our projects.

Kait is having some trouble with the sailor being closed off and not really in the mood ever to share any substantial thoughts about his career.

According to him, he was "forced" into this project by his agent.

That leaves Kait with some uphill battles each day, but I'm confident she'll do great either way.

"Maybe just flash your tits or something, then he'll open up," Mira snickers, and we roll our eyes at her.

"Yeah, then he would probably have me sent right back to America. I don't think he's ever seen a set of tits," Kait says, making us laugh.

God. What kind of dude is this?

Wendy is the only one of us who is following a female athlete. She's having a great time learning about the dynamics of beach volleyball and how her athlete works together with her teammate.

It's cool hearing about a sport that combines two athletes, like a petite team.

She's also gotten a nice tan since I last saw her. The Brazilian weather will help a girl out in that matter.

Mira is still enjoying the sunny weather and the beautiful men of the NFL in Texas.

"I've been thinking about our trip. What about the Caribbean?" Kait asks.

She's the planner of our group.

Tell Kait you've been thinking about seeing a movie or booking a new workout class, and everything will be fixed the next day.

Whenever we go somewhere, she's the one in charge, and we love her for it.

"That sounds amazing to me," I say, looking over a small pond of ducks in the park I've ended up in. Whenever I take a trip outside, I discover some new sights that make my heart a little fonder of London.

The others agree, meaning Kait will have a proposal for us with flights, hotels, and activities the next time we talk.

We're just waiting for the plan for the few classes and meetings with our supervisors, then we'll be all ready.

When we hang up and I go back to my apartment, my anger has simmered down.

This is just what I needed.

Talking with my friends and enjoying a Sunday-morning walk.

I decide to do some sightseeing, wanting to make the most of my time in London whilst I'm here.

I have the Vegas trip in under two weeks, and when that's all done, I'll be heading back to the US two weeks after that.

The time really is flying.

I spend my day exploring the city and checking off some of my boxes. Making a list of things I wanted to do whilst I'm here was the perfect plan for a day like this.

There are some attractions I really want to see before I go back.

The Harry Potter tour is one of them.

There's just something about that universe.

I want to take my time, though, so I'll save that for a later time when I can spend my whole day there.

When I spot an ad for The Dungeon, a horror experience, I think about Sebastian and how he would probably enjoy that, the horror freak.

I sigh.

I really wish Luke hadn't interrupted us yesterday.

Then I remember him skipping breakfast with me, as if he were shutting me out.

He could have made plans, but I feel like he would tell me, which leaves me to the conclusion that he's avoiding me altogether.

We could have been exploring these things together, but instead, he took the cowardly way out and avoided me.

Well, he won't be able to avoid me tonight.

~

I smile as I take in my reflection in the mirror.

I'm wearing a black dress that is tight across the chest and flows from the waist. I've paired it with textured stockings, gold earrings, and my necklace. I've curled my hair and added a touch of eyeliner, enhancing my eyes.

Game night is probably a laid-back affair, but I don't mind being a little overdressed.

I plan to make Sebastian sweat a little.

If he chickens out on us from one interruption of my dear brother, then I'll at least make him think twice about shutting me out.

The least he could do is talk to me about this; we could figure this out together instead of him being in his own head.

But no, he'd rather not eat breakfast with me and hide.

Yeah, I'm still bothered by that.

Our breakfasts have become my favourite time of day, so when he dropped that, it stung.

When I knock on his door, it's Dean who opens and his reaction is the exact thing I wanted.

"Oh, darling. You look ravishing," he says, kissing my cheek for good measure. I lean into him, probably a little more than necessary.

"Thank you, Dean. You don't look too bad yourself," I say, my smile sly as I walk into the apartment.

I greet Fredrick and Ian, who quickly stand when I come in. Their admiration is adorable, but the man I'm interested in doesn't seem too eager to greet me just yet.

I ignore Sebastian, who's standing behind the counter in the kitchen, taking my time greeting the guys.

I do have manners, so I bought a large plate of tapas-inspired dishes. I've made some chicken skewers and mini pizzas together with a variety of fruits and cold cuts.

When I'm all done with my greetings, I make my way over to Sebastian.

The look he gives me halts my steps.

He's clearly not happy with me.

He's leaning on the counter, gripping the edge with both hands as his eyes send daggers my way.

The usual playful smile is gone, and in its place is a scowl.

"Sebastian," I say, putting down the dish in front of him. I'm tempted to turn back around, but I decide against it, wanting to push.

He has no right to be angry at me.

He's the one backing away from us, not me.

It may be a little childish to use his friends to make him jealous, but it's not like I've done anything with them.

"Lily," he mutters.

I meet his stare, feeling like we're arguing without saying a word.

I'm tempted to call him on his bullshit right then and there, but with his friends in the room, that could get awkward.

Therefore, when I'm tired of our staring contest, I shake my head before turning to the boys, clapping my hands together.

"Shall we get started, boys?"

Chapter 17

Sebastian

I'm in hell.

That's the only place I can be, considering the fire of emotions running wild in my body.

I'm ready to fucking snap, tell the guys to get lost, and have a word with Lily.

I'd probably have a lot more to say than a word.

She's driving me fucking insane.

Turning up looking like a goddess.

Any other girl would probably feel overdressed in an outfit like that.

Lily loves being the centre of attention, and she is getting plenty of it.

The guys are fucking falling all over themselves, and Lily is all for it.

She's her usual flirty self, but she's adding a few light touches, making me feel muddled.

Whenever the boys joke, she'll laugh, sometimes leaning in to touch their shoulder.

The touch is friendly, but all I feel is raging jealousy.

Because of course, the only person she's not acting that way towards is me.

She's not even looking at me.

And I only have myself to blame for that.

I knew I was a fucking coward for skipping our breakfast. I don't know what I'll do or say to her whenever we're alone again.

I wanted to jump right back into where we were before Luke interrupted us yesterday, but part of me knew that wasn't a good idea.

Therefore, I avoided it altogether, saying I couldn't make it.

Now, Lily is making me pay for my actions.

It's her turn to deal the cards, and when she handles the deck like it's made for her, doing tricks no one before her has been able to, I look up at the ceiling.

She's so fucking sexy, and she knows it.

The guys are practically drooling while looking at her, and I can't really blame them, considering my own thoughts.

"Should we make this interesting, boys? Play a round of strip-poker?"

As soon as she says it, I speak.

"No."

But of course, the other fuckers are all for it.

I grumble under my breath, but they all agree that we live in a democracy and four against one win.

Lily deals the cards, wearing a smug expression on her face.

Soon enough, that expression is a full-on grin when she's kicking all our asses.

No wonder she wanted to play poker; she's outstanding at it.

We've all lost our socks and shirts, and Dean is down to his boxers, which is where I'm going to draw the fucking line.

Lily, on the other hand, hasn't taken off a single clothing item, which I'm thanking the heavens for.

It's bad enough having her gushing over the guys and their muscles.

Again, everyone except me, of course.

When Dean loses another round, I'm done.

"We'll stop right here," I say, not giving room for discussion.

Lily rolls her eyes at me.

Dean lifts his hands.

"I have no problem taking it all off," he says, winking at Lily.

She starts laughing, and I breathe hard, trying to control my temper.

Then she looks at me.

"Calm down, Sebastian. We're done. No reason to go all-out dragon over there."

I get up, needing some space, and storm into my bedroom.

I drag a hand through my hair and down my face.

I'm tempted to pick up the phone and call Luke right here and now.

Tell him about my feelings.

Get it out of the way so I can tell Lily how I really feel.

I'm dialing his number, but when it goes to voicemail, I'm feeling just as frustrated and lost as before.

I'm the host for Christ's sake, and here I am hiding away in my room like a moron over my feelings for a woman.

Not just any woman, though.

This is Lily.

The freaking girl of my dreams for as long as I can remember.

Eventually, I make my way out of the bedroom.

I don't realise just how much time has passed, but all the guys have left, and Lily is cleaning up the kitchen for me.

God, I really am the worst friend to all of them.

Storming off because I'm a mess and not saying bye to them. Lily is cleaning up the kitchen when I've done nothing to deserve her kindness tonight.

She doesn't say a word; just goes around tidying up, putting the leftovers in the fridge, wiping over the counter.

I stand here, observing her, wanting to say something but not knowing what.

When she can't take the silence anymore, she speaks.

"You know what, Sebastian? I get that this is hard for you, but so is it for me," she says, frustration evident in her tone.

"You think this is hard, Lily? I'm going fucking crazy, and I don't know what to do. What if I end up fucking all of this up, and it leads me to lose both you and Luke? Then what?"

She drops the cloth on the counter before looking at me.

"And what if you don't?" she asks, and again I'm left with the same feeling as when Dean told me to talk to Luke.

It all sounds so simple.

But this feels as far from simple as you can get.

I'm freaking terrified.

I swallow.

"I don't know, Lily," I mumble.

She takes a moment to look at me before something clicks in her expression.

I fucking hate it.

"Okay, then. Thank you for providing that clarity. I'll be going now. Goodnight, Sebastian."

She storms towards the door, and I'm left standing here, feeling like I just missed out on something great.

~

The next day, I have an early-morning practice, which means no breakfast with Lily.

I don't think I'm welcome in her apartment anyway. I tossed and turned all night, frustrated by the situation.

I really need to talk with Luke.

I can't go on like this.

I owe it to her, and to myself, to be honest with him.

If not, I'm going to lose my sanity.

When I'm in the elevator, on my way back to my apartment, my phone beeps.

Lily: Can you come over?

I haven't talked to her all day. I let her know I had an early practice, and she just said she would stay at home today. After that, it's been silent.

I've missed talking with her, even by text.

I've gotten accustomed to our routine, including texts throughout the day.

Small updates about what we're doing and making plans for the evening.

It's been less of that after my behaviour these past few days.

I get off the elevator on her floor and make my way to the door.

When she opens, I can tell something is wrong right away.

She's pale, and her eyes are glossy. She's wearing a big sweatshirt and some shorts, looking like something she'd wear to bed.

"Thank you for coming. I'm not feeling the best," she mumbles.

Then she falls into my arms, fainting.

I catch her, and when I feel her body temperature, I curse.

She's burning up, obviously running a high fever.

She's probably been sick all day, and she didn't even tell me.

I lay her on her side, checking that she's breathing normally as I call up Harriet.

She should be at my apartment.

"Hi, Harriet. Can you please come down to Lily's apartment? She just fainted, and she's burning up. Probably a fever," I tell her, and just a few seconds later, I hear the elevator doors opening.

When Lily stirs, I lay her across my legs, her head in my lap as I trail my fingers down her cheek. It takes a few seconds before her eyes open, and she looks a little hazy.

"Christ, Lily. Why didn't you tell me you're sick?" I ask her, feeling my heart pound in my chest.

What if I hadn't gotten here in time?

She could have hit her head when she fainted.

Harriet comes rushing out of the elevator, and I realise I didn't even get to close the front door before Lily fell into my arms.

"Oh, dear. How are you?" Harriet bends down to us, feeling her temperature as Lily mumbles something about being fine.

I shake my head at the beauty in my lap.

So stubborn and independent.

Fine my ass.

I hoist her up into my arms, bridal style, before I lay her down on the couch.

"Can you get some toiletries for her? I'll look for some clothes, then we'll bring her to my apartment," I tell Harriet.

When I've made sure Lily is okay on the couch, we get straight to work.

When I roam through Lily's wardrobe, I don't find anything that looks remotely comfortable.

Dresses, skirts, and jeans don't make for the comfiest fit when you're sick.

She'll have to borrow something from me.

When we have what we need, we make our way up to my apartment.

It may not be the wisest choice to move her, given her current state, but it will be easier to care for her from my space.

I have several bedrooms in my apartment, but I don't hesitate to bring her to my room.

I lay her carefully down in the bed before stroking some hair away from her face.

"I'm so hot, but I'm also freezing," she mumbles, her eyes half-open.

I help her under the duvet.

"It's your fever, Lily. I'll have someone come and examine you," I murmur.

"That's not necessary. It's probably just a cold, and I don't want to be even more of a hassle," she insists, but I don't bother arguing with her.

I can't believe she would say something like that.

She could never be a bother, and I'm angry at her for not telling me sooner that she was sick.

She fucking fainted in my arms.

She's already falling asleep; her body is tired from the infection.

As soon as she's asleep again, I'm calling a doctor.

"You're not a hassle. You're the light of my fucking day," I tell her, but she's already fast asleep.

I stay with her for a while, making sure she's okay, before I make my way out of the room and call a doctor.

Harriet is already cooking up chicken soup, which smells delicious.

"What happened?" she asks me when I enter the kitchen.

"She texted me, asked me to come to her apartment, and when I got there, she fainted in my arms. I haven't seen her all day, as I had an early morning practice, and she just said she was staying home."

I'm angry at myself for the distance between us. If things had been different between us, I would have known sooner.

Over the last few weeks, we've been texting throughout the day, but after the fiasco this weekend, it was the first day I hadn't talked to her much.

Now, I'm livid knowing she is sick, and she didn't even tell me before it got so bad.

"Something happened between you two? I thought she usually went with you to the stadium."

Harriet doesn't miss anything.

Considering the assholes I have as my friends and how effortlessly they flirted with Lily yesterday when they know I'm crazy for her, well… I won't be speaking with them about this.

They'll only give me more shit about not making a move.

Therefore, Harriet seems like the best option.

"I almost kissed her. And then I pulled away from her. She's the sister of my best friend, and I'm afraid of losing both of them if this doesn't work out."

Harriet thinks over what I just said, saying nothing for a while.

She may work as my chef, but Harriet has also become someone I ask for advice every now and then.

She's lived a colourful and exciting life, and whenever she shares her insights, I'm deeply grateful.

"Hm, that's tough, Sebastian James, but do you think you'll manage to stay away from her? I've seen you around her, you know, and I must say, I'm surprised you haven't kissed her, considering how you look at her."

I exhale.

Wherever I go, the people around me seem to know how I feel about this girl.

I may not have been as secretive about my feelings as I thought.

Harriet is right. I won't be able to stay away from her; I don't want to, either.

"Yeah, I won't. Right now, though, the priority is her health. I'll call her brother."

I get up and dial Luke's number, hoping he'll pick up.

Luckily, he does.

"Hey, man."

"Hey. I don't mean to spring this on you, but Lily is sick, and I was just wondering if she has a habit of fainting?" I ask him.

A cold or the flu shouldn't be too bad, but I don't like the fact that she fainted. As far as I know, that's not normal.

Hopefully, the doctor will be here soon.

"Yeah, she actually does. It's been many years, though, as far as I know. She can faint when she's stressed or running a high fever, or a combination of the two."

I drag a hand through my hair.

Hell, I bet our fight—if you can call it that—didn't exactly help the situation.

"Yeah, okay. A doctor is coming over soon. Anything else I should know?" I ask him, pacing around the hallway.

"She likes salty snacks and Coke with sugar when she's sick. Then she'll at least get some food in her system," he says.

"Okay, thanks. I'll make sure to get some," I tell him, writing it down so I don't forget.

My mind is reeling, consumed by concern and guilt.

I can't help but feel like she wouldn't have gotten so bad if she had told me sooner.

Her not telling me earlier has everything to do with my stupid behaviour yesterday.

And it's not like she has anyone else here in London to call.

"Take care of her, Sebastian. And call if there's anything."

"I will."

We hang up and the doctor arrives. I show him to the room and stand back when he examines her.

Lily stirs when he gently wakes her up.

"Hi Lily. I'm Dr. Davies. How are you feeling?"

She looks from the doctor to me before raising her eyebrows, and the fucking relief at seeing some of her attitude return is fantastic.

"Really? A doctor? I told you I probably have a cold."

"You fainted, Lily. Just let the doctor do his job, and he'll be on his way," I tell her.

She relaxes back in the bed and spreads out her arms.

"Check away." Making Dr. Davies and me chuckle.

Luckily, it seems like a regular flu, and the doctor tells me to watch her fever. It may be high for a few days, tiring her.

If she develops a cough or other symptoms, he told me to call. As soon as he's done with his checks, she falls back asleep, confirming what he just told me.

The most important thing is that she stays hydrated and eats something.

When he leaves, I sit down in the kitchen with Harriet, writing up a list of things I need for her.

"I'll go out and buy some snacks and drinks for her. Anything you need?"

Harriet is usually the one who does all the shopping, and the way she is smiling at me, it's clear she's having all sorts of ideas right now.

"What?" I ask.

"It's wonderful, Sebastian James. I just haven't seen this side to you before; it's delightful."

Her initial thoughts about this friend of mine coming to London and not being a friend at all are slowly coming true, if her expression is anything to go by.

I don't bother denying anything, knowing she's right.

Lily has never been just a friend to me.

~

I'm standing in the supermarket, realising how rare it is that I go food shopping.

Who knew there were so many types of snacks?

I'm contemplating which one to get and have just decided to buy a selection.

Hopefully, she likes some of them.

Next, I go over to the drinks section. Also, the choices are endless here.

By the time I'm done, the whole cart is full of all kinds of snacks, drinks, medicines, and fruit.

When I get back, I check on Lily, and she's having one of her wake-windows, so I bring her some soup and the snacks.

I sit down on the edge of the bed.

"How are you feeling?"

I'm tempted to grab her hand, but I realise she may not appreciate that, considering everything.

The priority now is her recovery.

"Tired, but a little better. I'm not as dizzy at least," she says.

I gesture to some of the snacks, and Lily starts laughing.

"What?" I ask, wondering if I got it all wrong.

What if she doesn't like anything?

"Did you buy the whole store?" she snickers, making me roll my eyes at her.

I didn't even bring everything I bought in; some of it is in the kitchen, but I may have gone a little overboard.

"I wanted you to have something you like," I tell her.

She sighs and gives me a beautiful smile.

I've missed having that smile aimed my way.

"Thank you, Sebastian. You're amazing," she tells me, making me feel like I might be the next one to faint.

Nothing feels as good as having her look at me in this way again.

She sips some of the soup, groaning.

"God, I think I might have to marry Harriet."

I chuckle.

She is a fantastic chef.

Chapter 18

Lily

I drift in and out of sleep, thinking I'm a little bit better, but then the fever will rise again, leaving me exhausted and ready for a nap once again.

When I wake up, the clock on the nightstand says it's almost midnight.

I look around, taking in the room, and only realise where I am.

I've never been in Sebastian's bedroom, but this must be it.

It's big and modern, but with hints of him all over.

To my right, it appears to be an entrance to a walk-in closet. He can't have that in his guest bedroom, can he?

Maybe he does.

As I noted when I got here, he is rich as fuck, which means he could have walk-in closets in every room.

But there are some other items in this room that confirm my suspicion.

His workout bag lies in the chair in the corner of the room. On the nightstand sits a book and a picture frame with none other than my brother and Sebastian.

It's a beautiful picture; they're smiling toward the camera with go-kart racing suits around their waist.

I remember this story.

Sebastian will never let Luke live down the fact that he, a Formula 1 driver, lost to him.

Those boys have been through a lot together, and I realise I may have been too hard on Sebastian over these last few days.

Wanting him to take that step, but not seeing it from his perspective.

I can tell he's struggling, wanting to do the right thing; it's one of the many qualities I adore about him. It's just frustrating when that prohibits him from starting anything with me.

I'm burning up again, and decide that a shower is needed.

Having a fever means taking clothes on and off all the time. I grab one of the t-shirts resting on top of the drawers.

It covers me past my butt, and smells like Sebastian.

When I make my way out to the living room, I'm not expecting to run into anyone.

I yelp when I spot Sebastian, shirtless, whilst he's watching TV.

"Why are you up this late? Don't you have practice tomorrow?"

He looks up at me, takes in my attire, and a small smile appear on his lips.

"Nice outfit," he murmurs.

It may be my fever playing games with me, but the playful, flirty Sebastian seems to be making an appearance.

After the last few days of strain and tension between us, it feels good.

I sit down on the couch, suddenly feeling very exposed with just the t-shirt, but it's not like he's wearing much either.

Just a pair of sweatpants.

"Shouldn't you be asleep?" I ask him again. As far as I know, he's no night owl, usually going to bed early.

"Couldn't sleep. How are you feeling?"

"A little better. I figured I could use a shower," I say, regretting it right away.

I don't want this moment to end.

It feels good just to be together, to talk again.

I've missed this—missed him.

"You go ahead and do that. I'll cook up some noodles. Sound okay?"

I nod, my head spinning on this whole day.

He's been wonderful.

Buying me snacks for the next year, by the looks of it.

Letting me sleep in his bed, leaving him in a guest room in his own home.

Calling the doctor to check up on me.

And now, he's going to cook for me.

Noodles may not be the hardest dish, but still. The gesture means a lot.

I get up and head for the shower.

Feeling the water run down my body is fantastic. When I spot my own shampoo, conditioner, and bodywash in the shower, my heart skips a beat.

Did he bring that as well?

He really thought about everything.

If I had a hard time resisting this man before, it won't get any easier if he keeps up these acts.

I finish the shower, grab a new t-shirt—courtesy of Sebastian—of course, and make my way back to the kitchen.

He's just putting out two bowls and an ice-cold Coke for me when I sit down.

"Is this a wild guess, or did you happen to know I prefer regular Coke when I'm sick?"

Usually, I'm a Coke Zero girl, but when I'm sick, I prefer the sugar.

"I called Luke earlier. He told me," he says as he takes the seat across from me.

Usually, the mention of my brother drives that wall right up.

Now, it just highlights another thoughtful action by Sebastian.

When Sebastian opens his own can of Coke—without sugar—but still, I gape at him.

"Sebastian James. What is happening? Are you planning on drinking a can of soda? I think you must be running a fever as well," I tease him.

He rolls his eyes, giving me a smirk.

"Some girl told me to live a little more, so I decided I should listen to her."

Christ.

I really shouldn't get all hot and bothered by such a small comment.

"Sounds like a fun girl," I whisper, feeling terrified that the playful man in front of me will retreat just as quickly as he came.

"Yeah, she is."

~

"I have to go now, Lily, but Harriet is home."

I might be dreaming.

It certainly feels like it.

Especially when I feel lips pressed to my forehead.

My body is heavy, and I snuggle more into the bed, soaking up the wonderful dream.

A while later, I wake up again. This time for real.

I turn towards the nightstand, going to grab my phone when I spot a small note.

- *I had to go to the stadium. I will be back later. Harriet is home.*

  S

Besides the note, a variety of drinks await, and I go for the peach iced tea. I may have teased him about his shopping spree, but it turned out quite well for me.

I get up and walk out to the kitchen, where Harriet is cooking up another lovely meal.

"How are you feeling, dear?" she asks, and when she heads straight to the kettle to boil some water, I realise how domestic my life has become here in London.

And how much I love it.

Harriet knows I like to enjoy a cup of tea with honey, usually after dinner with her.

Just like I know Sebastian will have the occasional cup of tea, but he favours a coffee cup.

Part of me feels sad that this adventure will end in just a few weeks.

"I'm feeling better. Thank you for taking care of me."

The sun is streaming in through the windows. One of the first days of sunshine, and I'm sick as a dog.

I must have done something to have this bad karma.

"Oh, dear. I haven't done much. Sebastian, on the other hand… I've never seen him like this."

I sigh.

"Yeah, he's been wonderful."

Him being the perfect caretaker isn't surprising. He's always thinking about others before himself and making sure the people around him are taken care of.

Harriet gives me a wistful smile, and we enjoy the meal she's prepared.

Later, Luke calls me while I'm sitting on the floor in front of the TV, trying to make some notes for the next interview with Sebastian.

We've had several already, and I think I already have more than enough for my paper, but I do want to cover all the themes.

The current state I'm in isn't producing the most useful schoolwork, so the break is appreciated.

"Hi, Luke."

"Hey, sissy. How are you feeling?"

I gather my stuff, putting it in the bag I picked up from my apartment earlier.

"I'm getting there. Should be back to top-tier health soon enough," I tell him.

I feel better than yesterday, but I still have a way to go.

"That's good. Sebastian, treating you all, right?"

Hell.

Right now, I'm glad this is a regular phone call and not a video call; then, I would have even bigger problems trying to hide my expression on the mention of his name.

I don't want to lie to him, and a part of me really wants to have a real shot with Sebastian.

That means my brother will have to be eased into this.

"Yeah, he's been like my own little caretaker," I say, feeling my heart pound in my chest.

I haven't even said anything that will cause any suspicion on his part about my feelings for his best friend, but I still feel like my heart can gallop straight out of my chest at any moment.

"That's good. I'm sure he's happy to do so for you," he says, making me curious.

"What do you mean by that?"

Luke chuckles on the other end.

"Nothing. Don't worry about it."

I want to dig so bad. My curiosity is killing me, but I don't want to be too obvious either.

What is my brother getting at?

Why is he being so cryptic all of a sudden?

Has Sebastian said anything?

I doubt it.

It's not like him to call Luke about me being sick and fainting and then drop the bomb on him that we almost kissed, but not to worry, since we haven't really been speaking after.

"I have a meeting, but feel better, Lily. I'll see you next weekend," he says, and we say our goodbyes.

Next weekend is Las Vegas, and I still don't know if Sebastian will be there.

I know it would mean a lot to Luke to have his best friend there.

Just as I'm heading out, Sebastian comes home.

"You leaving?" he asks, and there's no mistaking the disappointment in his voice.

"I thought I would get out of your hair. You've already done so much," I tell him.

I can't help but feel like a burden to him, especially when I've been sick.

"Nonsense. Please stay, Lily. Dinner will be ready soon, and Harriet will be offended if you don't eat with us."

I'd love nothing more.

"Okay, I'll stay. Can't offend Harriet," I say, even though I get the feeling that we both just want to spend more time together.

Chapter 19

Sebastian

Over the next few days, things go back to normal. Lily stays one more day in my apartment before she insists for the hundredth time to go back down to her flat.

I'm tempted to tell her that I don't want her to stay just because she's been sick; I just want her to stay.

These last few days have been good for us. It forced us to talk again, and with Lily being down and exhausted, she didn't have enough energy to argue with me.

So now, we're back to our routine of eating breakfast before going to the stadium and going home together for dinner with Harriet.

At least something good came out of her falling sick.

She wanted to attend my game on Wednesday, but after some conviction on my part, she stayed home and watched it on TV.

She still had a slight fever, and without someone watching her, I didn't want to risk her fainting again.

She called me dramatic, but I'll take that over having a scare like that again.

I've also made up with the guys.

Suppose I can call it that. It's not like we fought on game night, but my behaviour was uncalled for.

I was a moody bastard the whole evening, shooting daggers at them for looking and interacting with Lily.

When I mentioned it, they just laughed and told me they liked to rile me up. I'm not usually one who gets his temper going, so the guys saw this as the perfect opportunity to get under my skin.

Nevertheless, I apologised for being a dick.

After practice, I make my way to the office space I know Lily prefers.

Sometimes I'll look for her and find her in a new spot, but today, she's in the regular space, overlooking the field.

She beams when she sees me and starts packing up her stuff.

I'm reaching for her hand without even thinking, but luckily, she doesn't seem to notice before I've gathered myself and pulled it back.

The number of times I'll do something like that…

Reach for her hand, linger a little too long in a hug, or think about kissing her before catching myself.

I'm planning on doing all those things, but I need to talk to Luke first.

I finally got the clear to go to Vegas. It will be a short trip, but one worth making. This time, we're flying private to save some time as well.

I'm going to talk to him in Vegas—if I manage to make it that far before crossing the line.

Lily seems to understand my struggles without saying anything.

She'll flirt and be her usual cheerful self, but she seems to be thinking the same thing as me.

We will get there; we just need a little more time.

When we get back to the apartment, Harriet is ready with dinner. As always, it smells fantastic, and we set the table before sitting down.

We managed to complete one more interview for Lily's assignment today, and I must say, speaking with her is refreshing.

I've never had a mental coach or spoken to someone professionally—never really had the urge to do so—but I know several players who do and speak powerfully about it.

Talking with Lily is making me reflect more on things connected to my performance and what matters and does not.

Knowing her so well also works in my favour, as I find it easier to open up to her than to a stranger.

When dinner is all done, Harriet heads home, and for the first time in a week, it feels natural to ask Lily to stay for a movie again.

Such a small thing, but I've missed it dearly.

"No fucking horror movies, then I'm leaving," she says, making me chuckle.

After the fiasco of The Conjuring, I won't put on a horror movie, knowing she hates them.

It was fun scaring her though, also gave me a reason to touch her.

Christ.

I'm a starved man.

Having to scare a girl to have a reason to touch her. I really need to have that conversation with Luke.

We settle into the couch and find a documentary about a murder case.

Apparently, real murder is less scary than fake murder.

After a while, Lily gets up to grab a snack and some drinks.

She comes back with her usual Coke Zero.

For me, she's bought a glass of water with ice cubes and a Coke Zero. When she puts that down, she winks at me, which makes me chuckle.

She likes to tease me about living, but I appreciate the water, too.

I don't miss her sitting down closer to me when she drops back down on the sofa.

It would be so easy to drag her into my lap.

Before I can think too much about it, I do just that, her head resting against my chest.

"Scared, Bennet? Need me as support for the scary documentary?"

She gazes up at me.

I bring an arm around her.

"Yeah, something like that."

We watch the rest of the documentary, with Lily resting on my chest and me running my fingers occasionally down her arm.

It feels like the most natural embrace, having her in my lap.

When it nears the end, Lily sits up, bringing her legs on either side of mine and her arms around my neck.

I feel her weight on my thighs, and my body comes alive in seconds.

I swallow, looking into her eyes.

"Relax, I won't kiss you," she says, but her position is really testing my limits here.

"I'm already struggling here, and you're not helping the case, Lily," I tell her, resting my forehead against hers.

"We could just call Luke?" she suggests, and I'm tempted to do that.

Just get it over with.

"I need to do this in person in case he needs to get in a punch, you know," I say, half joking, half serious.

Lily hits me lightly in the chest.

"Don't say that."

I rest my hand on her lower back.

"Okay. A week then," she whispers.

"A week," I confirm.

Chapter 20

Lily

Putting a countdown on when we'll take the final step is like slow torture.

Every glance, touch, and moment together feels elevated. It doesn't help that Sebastian seems to be dealing with these frustrations much better than I am.

I'll give him a look of agony, and he'll just chuckle.

Having a crush on him when I didn't know if he had mutual feelings for me? Hard.

Having a crush on him and knowing he feels the same? Unbearable.

During the day, things are fine.

He comes down for our breakfast, and there will be some light touching, flirting—the usual.

Then we'll go to the stadium, and I won't see him for most of the day, which is good.

Being apart makes it easier not to want to kiss him senseless.

I still want that when we're apart as well, but the urge isn't as strong as when he's near.

Which brings me to the biggest challenge.

After our dinners with Harriet in the evenings, I'm struggling.

Like I am right now.

We're watching a movie—I have no idea which one. It could probably be a horror movie, and I wouldn't even notice.

My brain is high wired on all things Sebastian.

I feel like I'm going insane.

He's stroking my arm lightly, the most innocent touch, but it's making me feel feverish.

A very different fever from the one I was experiencing earlier this week.

I groan out loud, which makes Sebastian laugh.

That leaves me even more frustrated.

"Why is this so easy for you?" I sit up and look at him, all calm and collected, legs spread out on the couch.

"You think this is easy for me?" he asks, as controlled as ever.

"Well, yeah. You don't seem to struggle, and I'm about ready to fucking pounce on you," I say, not bothering to sugarcoat it.

When Sebastian moves closer to me on the couch and takes hold of my hand before whispering in my ear, I feel the goosebumps rise.

"You want to feel just how fucking hard this is for me?"

I barely get out a whispered yes before he moves both of our hands down his body. When he guides my hand to his crotch, I feel his hard length underneath my fingers.

I'm tempted to squeeze it, but Sebastian removes my hand just as I'm ready to play.

That quick feel of him is enough to make me feral for him.

These last few days really need to speed up.

"I'm in a constant state of want around you, Lily. But I've had some training in self-control over the years."

Years.

He's felt like this for years.

Just like I have.

"Years, huh?" I whisper back, giving him a small kiss behind his ear.

We're treading the line here, but I'm desperate.

"Yes, years, Lily. Therefore, I'll make it through these last few days, then we'll both get what we want."

Having him speak like that sends another wave of desire through my body.

He seems so confident, so sure, and it makes me wonder how he'll be in other ways as well.

He finally got the clearance that he could travel to Las Vegas with me, which means we're just a few days from telling Luke about us.

I can't fucking wait for that.

"So now be a good girl and lean back on this couch, while we watch this documentary, and I'll stroke your arm like we're just a couple of friends."

"Just a couple of friends," I grumble, making both of us laugh.

"At least for the next five days."

~

For the first time since we started our movie nights, we actually fell asleep. Sometimes I've fallen asleep only to wake later before heading back to my apartment.

Now, though, we both must have fallen asleep and cuddled together on the couch throughout the night.

I wake up in Sebastian's arms and snuggle closer to his body.

He's warm and wrapped all around me like a perfect blanket.

When the door opens, I expect it to be Harriet, so I don't move out of his arms.

She knows more than enough and probably won't be surprised to find us cuddled up together.

What I don't expect is Sebastian's whole family to enter the apartment.

His brother, mother, and father are all standing in the entrance, taking in the sight of their son and brother cuddling me.

"Well, well, well. Isn't this lovely?" Joseph, his older brother, exclaims.

I quickly try to pull out of his arms, but Sebastian is still half-asleep and tightens his hold on me.

"Sebastian, wake up!" I whisper-shout.

Oh my God.

At least I know them from growing up close to their house and from seeing Luke and Sebastian running around. Joseph is three years older than Sebastian, and five years older than me, so he was too cool to hang out with us.

Still, whether we're acquainted or not, this situation isn't ideal.

I finally manage to get out of Sebastian's hold and stand up.

At least we are fully clothed. Imagine if we had actually crossed that line and they found us naked.

Now, that would not be good.

"Lily! Such a pleasure to see you again."

His mother comes over and hugs me.

Finally, Sebastian wakes up.

Who knew he was such a heavy sleeper?

"Mom? Dad? Joseph? What's going on?" He rubs his eyes before standing up from the couch and greeting his family.

"We wanted to surprise you! But it seems like you surprised us," his mother says, the joy radiating off of her as she looks at me again.

God.

Why did we have to fall asleep this time?

His family seems to be getting all sorts of ideas about catching us snuggled together.

I don't know what to do or say, but Sebastian doesn't seem to be bothered by his family.

"Yeah, you all know Lily. She's doing her sports psychology project on me. We fell asleep watching a movie."

He makes it sound so domestic and friendly, which I'm grateful for.

It's also the truth.

His family doesn't seem to buy the story, though.

All wearing the biggest smiles I've seen.

"I should get going," I say, but they all protest right away.

Even Sebastian seems confused as to why I would want to leave this situation.

I'll definitely talk to him about this later, and how he would react if it were my family walking through that door.

He would probably have a panic attack right about now.

I don't have the will to argue with the four of them, though.

Breakfast with the Bennets it is.

Chapter 21

Sebastian

Having my family turn up was a pleasant surprise. Ever since I moved to London, I've gotten a little homesick at times, but these last few weeks with Lily have been amazing.

The loneliness hasn't been as prominent.

I glance over at her, happy to see her a little less rigid than before.

My family catching us all cuddled up together on the couch probably wasn't her ideal wakeup call.

I don't think I've ever seen her so panicked. She was adorable.

I couldn't really care less about them catching us.

My family has teased me about my crush on Lily ever since I first laid eyes on her.

They were all ecstatic to see me with her.

My mom is probably already planning our wedding in her head.

Lily doesn't know that, so she probably thought I would freak out about this as well.

As soon as that Las Vegas trip is done, I'll tell anyone willing to listen that she's mine.

Soon enough, Lily has warmed up and is her usual self, charming my whole family.

Even though they've met before, it's probably been a couple of years since they last saw her.

My parents hang on her every word, and Joseph watches me with a smirk.

He's been the one to tease me the most about my crush, and I can tell he's enjoying this.

I don't mind being teased by him. Soon enough, she will be mine.

Eventually, we have to get ready to leave for the stadium, and Lily says bye to my family before hurrying down to her apartment.

As soon as the door closes behind her, Joseph is all on me.

"Fucking finally, Sebastian!"

I roll my eyes.

"We're not together. At least not yet," I tell him, helping my parents clean up the kitchen.

"And why's that?" my dad asks.

They're all up in my dating business, it seems.

"I have to talk to Luke about this. And I want to do that in person, which I'll do in Vegas next week."

Mom sighs, still on a high of happiness. Lily has that effect on people.

"Oh, when he's having the biggest weekend of his life?" Joseph says.

Luke could win the championship in Las Vegas; that's why we're going.

"What? You think I shouldn't talk to him?"

Joseph shrugs his shoulders and says that it's essential that Luke is on top of his game.

Hell, maybe this is a bad idea.

I may wait until after the race.

That means three more days of fucking agony. But what's three more days in the big scheme of things?

~

The good thing about having my family visit is that it's easier to keep my hands off of Lily as we're not alone—ever.

That's equally as frustrating. I haven't had many moments alone with her after they arrived.

This is for the best for us.

This way, we'll be less tempted to cross that invincible line.

On Saturday, I'm packing up my bag for my game when my phone beeps.

Lily: Should I wear your jersey tonight? I don't know what your family will think.

Cute.

Again, they would probably be surprised if she didn't wear my jersey, as they're all going to be wearing the same thing.

The Bennet family is all out in the supporter attire.

Sebastian: Absolutely.

I say goodbye to my family and stand in the elevator when I decide to make a quick pit stop at her apartment.

I want a moment with her alone.

When she opens the door, she seems surprised to see me but happy, nevertheless.

As soon as I see the jersey across her body, I sport a similar smile to hers.

Seeing her in that outfit will always be a favourite.

"Nice outfit," I comment, making my way into her apartment.

"Thanks. It was rather expensive," she jokes.

She's wearing our home jersey.

I stand there, taking her in when Lily speaks again.

"Was there anything you wanted, Sebastian?" she asks huskily.

"There are lots of things I want, but they will have to wait. Preferably, after your brother wins that championship."

She groans and turns away from me, dragging a hand through her hair. She takes a few steps, creating distance between us.

"Okay, then. I can't look at you."

I can tell she's joking by her tone, but she's fighting the pull just like I am.

Ever since that countdown started, knowing we're close to getting what we want is the sweetest torture.

Craving.

Hope.

Desperation.

It's all there.

I go after her and decide that seven days are way too long.

I can't go a minute without knowing how her lips taste on mine.

"You know what? Fuck waiting."

I grab her around the elbow and pull her to me, crashing my lips to hers.

As soon as I kiss her, I can't believe that there was ever a time I could deny myself this.

She feels fucking perfect against me.

I circle my arms around her body, holding her tightly against me whilst I explore her mouth.

She kisses me back with the same determination, mumbling a "finally" against my lips as her hands grasp a hold of my hair.

I grab her around her thighs, lifting her, never breaking our kiss, before putting her down on the kitchen table.

"Fuck, Lily," I groan against her, coming up for some air before I kiss down her throat. She pulls me harder against her, eager for my touch.

When she moans my name, I nearly combust right on the spot.

It's like the most wonderful music ever.

A song you'll never tire of.

She pulls my face towards hers, smashing our lips together again as her hands grasp my face.

After what must be minutes, we break apart, our foreheads resting against each other.

"What happened to that precious self-control?" she whispers against me.

"Seeing you in my jersey again. I've never wanted to kiss you more than the first time I saw you in it," I tell her honestly.

I'll never forget that moment with her.

It was one of the first moments on this London adventure of hers, and I knew I stood no chance against my feelings for her.

"I thought I had scarred you for life that day. You looked terrified."

She presses her lips to mine again, and I bite her bottom lip before letting it go.

"Yeah, you terrified me alright. I've never wanted anyone as much as you when you so proudly sported my name across your back."

I give her one last lingering kiss; I'm already late.

"I'll see you later," I say, breathless and spent from finally having a taste of her.

"Yeah, you will. Go win a game—maybe even score a goal for me," she says, and I might have to go and do just that.

Chapter 22

Lily

I'm still sitting on the table Sebastian set me on top of, feeling my lips.

The lips he kissed.

After what has felt like an eternity.

Gosh.

Those butterflies have grown into full-on birds in my stomach, and they're flying all inside my body.

We fit so perfectly together, every touch and glide of our lips like a perfect set.

Who knew the jersey would push him over the edge?

I've worn it several times around him, but I guess the last few days have strained him as well.

Before his family showed up, we could at least have our small moments of touching and lingering. Not quite touching like we wanted to, but still having some form of intimacy.

That all became more difficult when his family showed up.

We haven't been alone these last few days, so I guess he felt as ravenous as I.

Worked out great if you ask me.

I want to call Jessica, but my dear brother might be close by, which could be a challenge.

She's been supportive every step of this journey ever since finding a breathtaking gown for the F1 gala months ago, when I knew Sebastian would be there.

I don't want her to have to keep secrets from her boyfriend though. And we're planning on talking to Luke soon enough.

I'm still feeling the high when my phone beeps, Joseph letting me know they're going down to the lobby now.

Shit.

I've been thinking about that kiss for thirty minutes.

I quickly gather my purse and lock up before meeting up with the family of the man who consumes my every thought.

~

We're watching the game, and Sebastian is bringing his best to the field.

He always does, but he seems a little extra pumped today.

I can tell that having his family support him means a lot to him.

His team wins the ball and starts advancing up the field. Sebastian just got passed the ball, and he looks around for an opening before sending it toward another player, before he runs the last stretch.

He's positioned inside the 16-metre perimeter, and when the ball comes flying towards him, he kicks it straight into the net.

I jump up from my seat, screaming out in excitement together with all the other fans around us. People are waving with their team scarves, the red and white spreading out in the stands. I probably won't have much of a voice left when I wake up tomorrow, but I don't care.

His mom is teary-eyed as she watches her son and his teammates gather around him.

Joseph and his dad are cheering loudly for him, too.

Experiencing this moment with his family feels perfect.

The rest of the game is equally as fun, and his team ends up winning 4-1.

After the game, Sebastian runs over to where we are seated.

His whole family hugs him, telling him how proud they are of him.

I stand back, watching the exchange and feeling my own emotions run high.

I know it's taken some sacrifices for him to get to this point. Leaving your home country must feel daunting.

Seeing him in this moment makes perfect sense. He's right where he belongs.

When he's done with his family, he comes over to me, and I feel my heart pounding in my chest—unsure how to act around him after things changed between us.

I really want to kiss him, but we're in a public space, and his family is right there; so instead, I hug him.

"I'm so proud of you," I murmur into his neck, standing on my tiptoes to reach as high as I can.

The noise around us seems to fade as I hug him tightly against me.

"Thank you. I really want to kiss you right now," he whispers, making me squeeze him a little harder.

"I know the feeling, but there are so many people here, not to mention your family."

We break apart, our hands still resting around each other. I don't want to let go of him just yet.

"Later, then," he says before he drops his arms around me.

I can't wait for later.

~

When we get back to the apartment, Dean is blowing up Sebastian's phone, telling him that he needs to go out and celebrate his great game with him and the guys.

Joseph is all for it, eager to experience London's nightlife.

I'm happy to do anything Sebastian wants.

He should celebrate. I'm always teasing him about living, and a night out with his mates seems like a good place to do that.

I'm putting away the clean dishes when I feel his arms around my waist.

He nuzzles into my neck.

"I don't think I want to ask you, because I think you'll say the same thing as the others, and I just want to stay here with you," he murmurs.

That does sound like a perfect option as well, but again, he should be with his teammates and his brother, who is leaving tomorrow.

I turn in his arms, happy to have a moment alone while Joseph gets ready in the bathroom and his parents have gone back to their hotel.

"You know how much I love our nights on that couch—and something tells me it would be even more satisfying than before—but yes, I do think you should go out. At least for a little while," I tell him.

He leans in, kissing me, and I press harder against him. His tongue twists with mine, and I whimper against him.

Staying in seems like the better option right now.

When someone clears their throat, we break apart and look over to Joseph, who's wearing a big smirk as he takes in the sight in front of him.

We still have our arms around each other and are breathing heavy from our make-out session.

"Leaves you alone for five minutes and finds you with your tongues down each other's throats," he chuckles, and I blush.

We haven't exactly told anyone about this; we just kissed for the first time today.

It feels all so new, even though we've wanted this for a long time.

Again, Sebastian doesn't seem fazed by being caught by his brother, just like when they first arrived and found us cuddled up together on that couch.

He either has no shame or his relationship with me isn't that surprising to them.

We haven't exactly talked about it, at least not with me around. I feel like we're in limbo until we've spoken to Luke.

"If you got a problem with that, you can find yourself another place to stay."

Sebastian shrugs, before he presses his lips to my cheek.

Gosh.

I like this Sebastian—a lot. He's unapologetic and affectionate.

"Go get ready, lovebirds. We have a town to conquer."

Chapter 23

Sebastian

I'm seated at a table, watching Lily dance her ass off on the dancefloor; and even though I hate to admit it, Dean was right.

It's fun having a night out, especially when Lily is dancing and singing her heart out. She's magnificent and sexy all at once.

I'll gladly go out again if it means seeing her enjoy herself this much.

Occasionally, a dude will saunter up to her, but she'll give them a look, say something, and they'll be on their merry way.

Each time, I'm up on my feet; but by the time I've taken two steps, they're already gone.

She's handling herself just fine.

And she's looking at me, all sinful eyes and hidden smiles.

"Please tell me you've made a move, because watching the two of you right now is messed up if you haven't," Dean says beside me, sipping on his water.

We're not drinking as it's the middle of the season, and neither of us fancies a hangover.

Fredrick is out on the dancefloor, cosying up to a girl he'll probably bring home for the night.

Ian is off playing darts whilst I, Dean, and Joseph are hanging back, watching the action unfold in front of us.

Or, for me, watching Lily.

"I caught them with their tongues so far down each other's throats, I'm surprised they're still breathing," Joseph says, snickering, which makes Dean laugh as well.

"It wasn't that bad, you idiot," I say, but it probably was.

Now that we've crossed that line, I'm not that interested in holding back.

And to my defence, I thought we were alone.

Lily was more horrified than I.

I think it was the first time I've ever seen her blush.

She's usually a happy-go-lucky type who doesn't care what anyone has to say about her.

It's one of the things I love about her.

But having Joseph interrupt us?

She was embarrassed, which I found adorable.

I should probably tell her about my family knowing about my crush on her for a long time, but it's also fun watching her squirm a little.

She's been making me feel unbalanced in her presence these past weeks—joking about seducing my coach, and asking me if I ever have sex with girls.

Therefore, she can handle blushing around my family.

"I'm happy for you, man, and you suit each other," Dean says, looking over to where Lily is dancing.

She's found herself a group of girls who are belting out the lyrics to "Club Can't Handle Me."

She's stunning.

"Yeah, I'm just hoping her brother won't kill me," I say.

"Luke is a good guy. I don't think he'll be that angry. And are you sure he doesn't already know? It's been obvious for us at least—how you feel about her," Joseph says.

Luke has mentioned Lily having a crush on me, but each time I've felt panicked, not knowing how to react.

He's always said she had a crush on me, but he's never suggested that he knew that I also liked her.

I've also not been seeing her regularly as I have in these last few weeks.

Those feelings and the crush have intensified massively by spending time with her.

Before I was able to push it to the back of my mind, not feeling the need to talk to Luke about it, as I wasn't ever planning on doing anything about it.

Now, the situation is very different.

Joseph does have a point, though.

My whole family wasn't all that surprised to see us cuddled up on the couch.

Maybe Luke will have a similar reaction.

At least I can hope.

Lily comes over after her sing-along marathon, and when she sits down in the booth next to me, I place my hand on her thigh.

Her bare thigh.

I drag my fingers up and down her leg, each time going a little higher.

Lily continues talking with Dean and Joseph as usual, seemingly unaffected by my touch.

I watch her reactions, and when she squeezes her legs a little tighter together, her breathing deepening, I push her more.

Let's see just how much she'll allow me to do in this public place.

It's not like anyone can see my hand; we're hidden in the dark, but we're still not alone.

I bring my fingers to the inside of her thigh, nearing her underwear.

"Are you enjoying London? Or would you have liked to have stayed back in Seattle?" Josep asks Lily.

I bring my fingers higher, feeling the lace of her underwear.

Lily adjusts in her seat, and I expect her to close her legs, break my touch.

I should know that Lily would never back down from a challenge.

She spreads her legs further apart, giving me better access as she answers Joseph.

"I'm glad I ended up in London. I don't think Seattle would have been as satisfactory or thrilling," she says, and the irony isn't lost on me.

She fucking loves this.

I bring my fingers inside her thong, and when I find her wet from my touch, I'm tempted to bring her with me to a more private place to finish this off.

The first time I have my fingers in her cunt, and we're in a fucking bar.

We're nothing but adventurous.

It does feel like us, though.

Always up for a challenge. A little forbidden and daring.

I bring my finger inside her, and the sensations running through my body are so intense you would think I am the one being touched.

Fuck.

We really shouldn't be doing this.

But the kick of it makes it all the better.

Lily leans slightly forward, my touch making her breath harder as I push my finger in and out of her.

"I want to play a game of pool. Anyone up for it?" Dean asks, and luckily for us, Joseph volunteers to go with him whilst we stay back.

They probably think we want to make out some more, and we might do that as well, but if only they knew what we are doing right now.

When they leave, Lily doesn't contain her reactions to my touch as much.

She lets out a whimper as I lean down, kissing her throat as I continue working my finger inside her.

"Fuck, Sebastian. We shouldn't," she whispers, biting her lip.

When I catch her eyes, they tell me all I need to know, together with the way her body is responding to my touch.

I add a second finger, whilst I start circling her clit with my thumb.

"Hell. You even told me you were a filthy girl, Lily. I didn't realise just how much," I say, kissing her.

"Sebastian." My name is a plea on her lips, making my cock hard from her sounds and reactions.

She rests her head against my shoulder, and when I feel a bite to my throat, I feel fucking feral for her. She's trying to contain her sounds against me.

Christ.

How explosive will we be in bed and with privacy?

"Let go, Lily," I tell her, feeling her walls tighten around my fingers as she comes.

She lets out a small moan, which has my body tensed up.

I just gave her an orgasm in a bar—the first one of many.

We're both doomed.

"Fuck. I knew you could be wild, Sebastian. Happy to have brought out that side of you around me for once," she says, happiness radiating off her.

I withdraw my fingers, licking them clean of her arousal.

Lily watches me, her lustful gaze intense.

"Yeah, I feel fucking wild around you," I tell her.

It's like she's unleashed a beast.

She's consuming me, but I'm welcoming it.

"Can we go home?" she asks. I'd want nothing more than finishing what we just started back at my place, but Joseph is staying with me, complicating things.

We could go to her apartment.

"Joseph is staying at my place. We can go to yours, but then you'll have to be ready for a lot of teasing from him tomorrow," I tell her.

He would definitely know why I'd rather spend the night with Lily.

"Or you could just sneak out, like my dirty little secret."

She smirks at me.

Hell.

The suggestion is tempting, but I want to savour her. Not feel rushed to get back to my place, to avoid suspicion.

I want our first time together to be perfect.

"I plan on taking my time with you, Lily. Therefore, we'll wait till he leaves. That's one of the things we do best—wait," I tell her, leaning in to kiss her.

She sighs against my lips, frustrated but agreeable.

"I'll book Joseph on the next flight out of London," she says, making us laugh.

I know the wait will make it that much sweeter.

~

We finally get Joseph to agree it's time to go home. He's a little drunk, and I help steady him as we make our way into my apartment.

When he's all down for the night in one of the guest bedrooms, I make my way down to Lily's apartment.

I want to give her at least a proper goodnight.

When she opens the door, she's just in her stockings and underwear, her dress thrown over one of the chairs.

I swallow, taking her in.

She stands there, confident and sexy in the moonlight.

Maybe this wasn't a good idea.

Looking at her, the idea of going back up to my own apartment seems like a terrible idea.

I close the distance between us, pulling her to me as I kiss her.

"Fuck, maybe waiting is overrated," I murmur against her lips, making her chuckle.

She drags her hands under my t-shirt before she takes it off.

"We'll wait, Sebastian. But I'll give you something to help release the pressure," she husks against my lips before she starts kissing down my body.

The sight in itself is arousing—add the fact that she's half naked—and I might come from the sight of her alone.

When Lily gets to my pants, she unzips my trousers before dragging them down over my ass.

I've been hard for what feels like hours.

It has everything to do with her.

She kisses my length through the fabric of my boxers, gazing up at me with lustful eyes.

Lily seems to be enjoying this just as much as I am.

Next, she pulls down my boxers, finally freeing my cock.

She looks at me before she licks her lips.

Then, she grabs a hold of my cock, kissing the tip and licking off the pre-cum that's leaking.

I grab a hold of her hair, needing something to steady myself.

When she brings my cock all the way into her mouth, I groan out loud.

"Fuck, Lily."

She starts sucking me off, taking as much of my length as she can muster.

She brings her hand to the backside of my thighs, pushing me against her, urging me to take control of the pace.

I start fucking her mouth, loving the feel of her slick lips around me as she works me in and out of her mouth.

I'm worried I'm being too rough, but then Lily starts playing with my balls, which causes me to grunt and moan as she makes me feel amazing.

When I'm nearing the edge, I warn her, but Lily only seems more eager to continue pleasuring me.

"Lily, I'm going to come," I tell her.

She sucks even harder, making me shoot my cum straight down her throat.

Lily swallows every single drop, and when I come down from my orgasm, breathing heavy, she slaps my pecks.

"You should sleep better now, babe."

Christ.

I don't know what I expected from Lily in a sexual regard.

Maybe that she would be a little more timid?

I'm quickly learning never to underestimate her.

She's herself in and out of the bedroom.

Her confidence, her sparkling personality, and her boldness are all there.

She's my match in every fucking way.

"Come here," I say, dragging her to me.

I kiss her, not caring that she just had my cock in her mouth.

She kisses me back with the same passion, our hands touching every possible inch of skin.

I start working my way down her body, kissing, nibbling, and biting as I go.

Lily pushes herself against me, urging me on.

When I get to her hips, I pull down her thong, exposing her cunt to me.

My hands go around her body, pushing her against the windows to steady her.

I look up at her, already finding her eyes trained on me, down on my knees, fucking desperate to taste her.

"You're glorious, Lily," I tell her, before sinking my tongue into her heat, not breaking our eye contact.

Lily moans at the contact, her hand finding my hair as she uses the other one to hold herself against the window.

"Fuck, Sebastian, that feels amazing," she says, her head falling back against the window as I lift her leg over my shoulder, giving me better access.

Her body is so responsive, making me hard all over again from having her at my mercy.

I work my tongue in and out of her before I add a finger to heighten her pleasure.

Lily is wild against me, making me feel drunk on her taste and sounds.

I feel her tightening around me, and I grab her ass roughly in my hands as I send her over the edge.

Riding out her orgasm on my fingers and tongue, her breathing calms as I look up at her.

She gives me a lazy smile, the happiness evident on her face.

I kiss up her body, mingling a little on her breasts, which earns me a chuckle from Lily.

"We really need to stop this if we're not going all the way," she murmurs, and even though it feels like torture, she does have a point.

I make my way up her throat before finally bringing my lips to hers once again.

Her arms go around my neck, tugging lightly at the hair in my neck as my tongue twists against hers.

We break apart, our foreheads resting against each other.

"Yeah, I should probably go before this goes any further," I say.

I'm tempted to carry her to the bedroom, finish what we've started, but I meant what I said.

I want us to have all the time we need, and I don't want to treat her like a hook-up and leave her after we've had sex.

I know Lily wouldn't see it that way, but I want to wake up with her when we take that final step.

Sneaking out like her dirty little secret, as she said, is not happening.

With one last lingering kiss, I step out of her embrace, pulling my boxers and pants back up.

I find my shirt scattered across the room, and when I look over at Lily, she's watching me, not caring to put on any clothes.

She's sexy as sin.

"Goodnight, Sebastian," she says.

"Goodnight, Lily."

Chapter 24

Lily

I wake up feeling more rested and relaxed than I have for a long time.

Yesterday was quite the night.

It makes me light-headed thinking about it.

Being with Sebastian was everything I've wanted and more.

He's already been the best lover I've ever had, and we haven't even gone all the way.

I don't have the most experience in the sexual department, but I've had a few partners over the years.

None of them have made me feel the way Sebastian did.

With other guys, they've made me feel like I'm too much, too demanding in the bedroom whenever I've voiced my desires or wanted to try something new.

With Sebastian, it was the total opposite.

When he was down on his knees, he looked intoxicated by me. Like this was the best time he's ever had, pleasuring me.

He makes me feel empowered and sexy, and I don't feel the need to hide from him or my desires.

I make my way out of bed, taking a quick shower and getting dressed in a pair of jeans and a sweater.

I grab my phone and smile when I see a text from Sebastian waiting.

Sebastian: Come up for breakfast

Lily: And what if I already have breakfast plans?

I obviously don't, but I like flirting with him. My social circle is basically limited to him here in London.

Sebastian: Cancel them.

Lily: So bossy.

Sebastian: You love it.

Yeah, I do.

Just as I'm heading out the door, my phone rings; it's the Sunday catch-up call with the girls.

Shit. I forgot about that.

I text Sebastian that I will be up after my call, but they don't need to wait for me.

I sit down on the couch, excited to talk to my girls and hear the latest developments.

Right away, Mira goes into a rant about the project and how she might have to stay in Texas for longer.

The project started well, but now, the team she's following has been too busy for her, leaving her with less data than she needs.

When she raised the challenges, she was told she could stay longer.

"It's just so frustrating. They agreed to this project, and now I feel like they're pulling out on me halfway," she says, pacing around her hotel room.

Not everyone has been as lucky as I have and has gotten their own apartment for this project.

Sebastian truly is the best host in every way.

"Maybe you can come to Australia. Help me out with the sailor," Kait says.

She's still not making much progress, which leaves her with similar challenges to Mira.

Not having enough data will make the writing more difficult, since our assignment is meant to build on it.

Wendy seems to be doing well, like me. I feel bad for Mira and Kait, though; school work is challenging enough as it is.

You don't need your athletes giving you a hard time on top of that.

"And if I have to stay longer, our trip to the Caribbean may be ruined, or at least shortened!" Mira says.

Kait blows out a breath, probably seeing her well-planned proposals fly out the window.

"Yeah, maybe we have to wing it. I know you're going to have a heart attack, Kait, but Australia does have nice hospitals, right?" I joke.

The others laugh, and I'm grateful to at least be able to put a smile on their faces even when they're going through something stressful.

We decide to wait with booking anything.

Hopefully, things will work out for the girls, and we'll be able to take our trip.

After saying our goodbyes, I make my way to Sebastian's apartment.

Joseph is seated at the table, his head in his hands, groaning. He's sporting a real good hangover.

I feel extra grateful for not drinking yesterday when I see his agony.

"A beautiful Sunday morning, isn't it, Joseph?" I say, mocking him a little.

Sebastian is putting out all kinds of food on the table. It looks like he's ordered breakfast for his whole football team when it's us three plus his parents if they come over.

Sebastian makes his way over to me, pulling me close to him before dipping down and kissing me.

I sigh against his lips.

Gosh, I'll never tire of this man and the feelings he evokes in me.

"Morning, babe," he says.

"Morning, babe," I murmur back, earning me a dazzling smile and a quick squeeze to my ass.

Sebastian really is an ass man.

I help him set out the plates, and just as everything is ready, his parents arrive.

"It smells lovely in here!" his mother exclaims as they enter the apartment.

His parents give both Sebastian and me hugs whilst his mother shakes her head at her eldest son.

"Joseph, how much did you have to drink last night? Would have thought you were the one scoring a goal and winning the match."

She ruffles his hair, Joseph muttering in his seat about a headache.

Sebastian's mom looks at him, pride in her eyes. He always plays marvellously, but having his family in the stands yesterday was something else.

He was spectacular.

I love watching him play; experiencing it together with his family was even better.

All were wearing his jersey and cheering him on.

"We'll come back for your quarter-final," his dad says, referring to the Champions League and our hope that his team will make it as far as possible.

His dad seems unwavering in his belief that they'll stand at the top at the end of the season.

They have a few games left before they'll advance to the quarter-final—if they continue playing as well as they've done this far.

At the mention of this, I feel a pit in the bottom of my stomach.

What will happen when I go back to the US?

We have only a few weeks left before I return to my life in Seattle.

Will we do a long-distance relationship?

Is this even a relationship?

I should probably talk to Sebastian about these things, but I'm worried about what he'll say.

Scared he'll say this is a temporary situation.

Fucking terrified if he tells me it's not.

I've had some flings, but those have been casual. Not really anything I've spent much time dwelling on, wondering about what we are.

Whenever my friends have talked about the need to define something between them and their man, I've never felt the need.

Going with the flow and not worrying too much has always been my strategy.

As I look over to Sebastian, I know deep down that I won't be able to handle this the same way.

I don't know if I even want to.

And he's been persistent about talking to Luke; that must indicate this is more to him than a fling, right?

Shit.

This is way too heavy to think about on a Sunday morning whilst having breakfast with his family.

These worries can rest for another day.

~

"I can't take any more."

Joseph is still hungover and complaining as we walk around the Sky Garden.

When Sebastian suggested it, I raised an eyebrow at him, knowing it's part of my bucket list.

Has he seen the list?

As I think about it, he's ticked off several of the things I've set out to do whilst I'm here.

His mom also seemed delighted at the idea, and soon enough, we were on our way.

Joseph would have a better time if he stayed back in the apartment, but their parents were insistent on some family time before they left.

That also included me.

When I stood up after breakfast, ready to give them some time alone, his mother gave me a stern look and asked where I thought I was going.

Sebastian just sat there wearing his signature smirk.

He seems to enjoy himself whenever I squirm around his family.

I stop when I spot several butterflies on the plants next to me.

Their colours are vibrant shades of blue, yellow, and orange. They're breathtaking.

Hands sneak around my waist as Sebastian stands behind me, resting his head on my shoulder.

"Having a good time?" He kisses my cheek, making my insides turn to mush.

I rest my hands on top of his, soaking in his presence.

"Yeah, it's beautiful here," I say, leaning into his body, letting his warmth enwrap me.

We stand there, watching the butterflies as they fly around.

"Do you think a drink will solve my hangover?" Joseph says from beside us.

"Spoken like a true alcoholic," Sebastian jokes, making me chuckle as well.

I didn't realise how much he had to drink yesterday, but I was rather occupied with Sebastian getting me off under the freaking table to notice.

I can't believe we did that.

That's what you get when you have two people who never back down from a challenge.

I wanted to see how far Sebastian would push it. I didn't think he would actually go as far as he did.

It was bloody fantastic.

I knew his wild side was in there, and I've been waiting for him to come out and play.

Joseph sets off for the restaurant, and we decide to tag along to get something to drink as well—preferably a coffee or a Coke Zero for me.

When Sebastian grabs my hand, those butterflies seem to have taken flight inside of me.

Such a simple gesture, but it lights me up.

His thumb caresses my hand as we order our drinks.

Joseph settles on some water, as does Sebastian. His parents and I order coffee.

"The only other grown-up here is you, Lily," his dad says, gesturing to the cup in my hand.

The playfulness of their family is wonderful.

"Yeah, the day isn't the same without some caffeine," I say, and his parents nod their heads in agreement.

This day is quickly becoming another great day, which seems to be the norm of this life I'm living in London.

Chapter 25

Sebastian

"I would tell you to take care, Sebastian, but I'm happy to see that you have someone else also taking care of you," my mom says, smiling at me as I hug her.

Ever since they saw me and Lily all cuddled up together, they've been soaring on a cloud, happy to see their son with someone they adore.

These last few days have been amazing—seeing her around my family, so effortlessly fitting in with them.

I've driven them to the airport, and even though I'm sad to see them leave, it doesn't feel as heavy as usual, knowing Lily is back in her apartment.

"Yeah, I'm doing good," I tell her, my dad taking her place, hugging me.

"We'll be back soon, son," he says, clapping me on my back.

Next up is Joseph, who eventually got over his hangover. He'll reconsider going out again for quite some time.

"Bye, lil bro. It's been a blast. Say hi to Lily for me and tell her that if she ever wants the better Bennet brother, I'm ready for her."

I hit him on his shoulder, probably a little harder than he expects, but he laughs, nevertheless.

"Won't be happening, you asshole."

He pulls me in for a hug, and I let him, considering I won't see him for a while.

My family wanders into the departure part of the airport, and I start making my way back to my car when I get a text from Dean.

He's sent me a link to an article, and when I open it, I stop in my tracks.

Fuck.

This cannot be happening.

Right in front of me is an article featuring Lily and me.

The headline says "Sebastian Bennet. Cosying Up to Mystery Woman", followed by a picture of us from today.

My hands are around her at the Sky Garden as we look out over the conservatory.

At least her identity isn't known yet.

It's only a matter of time, though.

The British gossip media is brutal.

Just as I finish the article, Dean sends me three more, making me groan out loud.

They're all from British and European news sites, but I wouldn't be surprised if this has reached the American media as well.

I really need to call Luke.

I hurry back to my car, considering whether to wait for the call and do it with Lily.

I decide against it.

If Luke tells me to stay away from her, I know she would jump in and tell her brother to back off.

Even though I'm not planning to do that, I still feel compelled to do this as right as possible.

It wasn't supposed to go down like this, but I can't help myself around her.

Not once did I think about the possibility of us being photographed. I was too occupied having a great time with both her and my family.

Hopefully, I'll at least get a hold of Luke before someone else tells him, or he sees an article himself.

My heart is pounding in my chest, and my hands get sweaty as I search for Luke on my phone.

Hell, it feels like I'm having a heart attack.

I hit call, bringing my knuckles to my mouth as I bite down, trying to calm my nerves.

Luke answers, and I don't know if I should feel relieved or not when he answers in his usual tone.

"Hey, man."

I don't think he knows, which I'm grateful for, but it makes it that much harder to come clean.

"Hey, Luke," I say, trying to sound as natural as I can, with my heart hammering so hard, I feel the pulse in my ears.

"I have something I need to tell you, and I don't know how, and it wasn't supposed to go down like this," I begin, my words rushing out in a panic.

Luke doesn't say anything, which only heightens my stress.

Who knew telling your best friend that you have feelings for his sister could be this nerve-wracking?

All my nervous experiences are lining up nicely; all linked to the beautiful blonde.

"Fuck, this is difficult. I'm sorry, I'm not making any sense right now. My head is a mess."

Luke is still silent on the other end.

Why doesn't he say something?

Probably because I'm a freaking mess and he's letting me get whatever I need off my chest before he gives his input.

"I like your sister," I say, holding my breath before I add,

"A lot."

Using the word like feels so juvenile, but I don't know how to put this.

I hadn't exactly planned what I was going to tell Luke, thinking I had a few more days to prepare for this talk.

Luke starts chuckling on the other end, and I exhale my breath.

"You think I didn't know?" he asks, amusement clear in his voice.

Fuck.

Okay.

This may be alright.

At least he's not mad… yet.

"You saw the articles?" I ask sheepishly.

Maybe I was too slow after all.

"What articles?" he asks.

Okay, then how did he know?

I drag a hand through my hair and explain the articles.

"I haven't seen them, Sebastian. But I've seen the way you look at Lily. Figured when you were going to spend so much time together in London, it was bound to happen. How long has this been going on for?"

It feels weird to talk about this with him, but at the same time, he is my best friend, and all I've wanted is for this to be okay.

That both my friendship with him and my relationship with Lily will be okay.

I realise we kissed for the first time yesterday, before my game.

Christ, we've already experienced so much together.

We may have kissed for the first time yesterday, but our connections have been growing ever since we boarded that plane across the Atlantic.

"I kissed her yesterday," I mumble, feeling like a child getting a scolding even though Luke hasn't been anything but supportive.

I should have known.

Luke is a great guy, and he's had his fair share of women's trouble with Jessica, which I've supported him through.

Still, this is his sister we're talking about.

"Yesterday, huh? Took you long enough, Bennet," he says, and my nerves start to settle.

The relief of having his approval, even support, makes the emotion thick in my throat.

"You are okay with this? I've been going fucking crazy, Luke. Worried you'd kill me, or worse, not want to be my best friend anymore," I tell him, feeling more vulnerable than I ever have.

"Man, I know you're a good guy—hell, the best I know. There's no one I would trust my sister with more. That being said, I'll fucking kill you if you ever hurt her," he says, and even though I know he's joking, I take his threat to heart.

"It's noted, boss," I joke, making both of us chuckle.

I start driving back to my apartment, still having Luke on the phone, but through the hands-free system.

We talk about the upcoming race weekend, which can be a monumental moment in his career.

I tell Luke that I haven't said anything sooner because of the race. I want him to be on top of his game, ready to bring home that title.

"I'm always on top of my game. You really need to start thinking more of yourself, Bennet."

Sometimes the Hastings siblings are very similar, like right now.

With Luke telling me how I should put myself first sometimes, too.

Lily has been telling me the same thing, pushing me to just do.

Do the things I want to.

Don't worry too much about what others will think.

Having Luke say the same thing means a lot, knowing I have his back.

"I'm excited for this weekend. We'll land on Thursday morning."

I'm already pushing it, going to Las Vegas when we're in the middle of the season, but luckily, the timing is good.

We have the weekend off, and as long as I'm back by Sunday night, it's all good.

Thankfully, the Las Vegas race is the only one taking place on a Saturday, which is perfect for me.

This time, we're flying private, which also saves us a lot of time.

"Yeah. It will be good to have you all here." Luke and Lily's parents are also coming to the race, all of us anticipating the win.

I'm sure Luke is feeling the nerves ahead of the weekend, but I'm also confident he'll triumph in this.

If something goes wrong, he will have another chance at the next race.

When we end the call, I've reached my parking spot at my condo.

I lean back in my seat, exhaling a long breath.

Now he knows, and he's okay with it.

Hell, he's had his suspicions, waiting for this.

It feels like a burden has been lifted from my shoulders.

I lock my car and go straight to her apartment.

I don't bother knocking, knowing she never locks her door during the day.

When I enter her apartment, Lily casts me a look from the kitchen, where she's preparing a cup of tea.

"I'm making tea, would you like—"

She doesn't get the chance to finish her question as I drag her against me, slamming my lips down on hers.

She's surprised by my hunger but kisses me back.

When we break apart, she gives me a dazzling smile.

"I love the passion, babe, but is there a reason for this pleasant attack?" she asks.

She's her usual vibrant self, meaning she probably hasn't seen the articles.

Or she doesn't care. That could also be the case.

"I spoke to Luke," I tell her, which brings a glimmer of panic into her eyes.

"Shit, why? I mean, we were going to talk to him, but I didn't think we would do it yet," she says.

I love that she says "we."

We are going to be just fine.

I wrap my arms around her, bringing her closer.

"He's on the first jet out, ready to murder me, so if you want a piece, you'll have to be quick," I tell her, squeezing her butt.

She rolls her eyes, slapping my chest lightly.

"Sebastian," she murmurs, curious to know what her brother actually said.

"He took it well. He said he had his suspicions already," I tell her.

Lily thinks that over.

"Yeah, I think he had. He said something when I was on the phone with him when I was sick."

Now I'm the curious one.

Lily blushes, which she rarely does, spiking my curiosity even more.

She goes back to preparing her tea, casting her eyes down to her assignment at hand.

"What did he say, Lily?" I ask, standing behind her, nuzzling behind her ear.

"He said he wasn't surprised you'd been the perfect caretaker, and that he thought you wouldn't mind at all," she mumbles, feeling shy all of a sudden.

"You think your brother is wrong, babe?" I tease her.

Taking care of Lily was no problem.

I was angrier about her not telling me that she was feeling ill than spending time getting her back into shape.

"I don't know—you tell me," she says.

I turn her around, wanting to look into her eyes, make her see that I'm serious about this; about her.

"He's right. I didn't mind taking care of you. After the shit you pulled on game night, I was grateful not to have to fight with you, and it gave me a reason to spend time with you," I tell her, looking into her eyes.

She smiles up at me.

"I think game night was fun," she says, pressing a quick kiss to my cheek before leaning into my ear.

"You were quite broody that night, Bennet," she whispers.

"Yeah, you made me crazy."

Still do.

Crazy about her.

Chapter 26

Lily

The look Sebastian is giving me right now nearly sends me into cardiac arrest.

There's so much in those eyes.

The relief is clear.

I was worried about my brother and how he would react to us, but I don't think my burden compares to the one Sebastian was carrying.

Then there's the desire that always seems to be humming between us.

On top of that, there's something more simmering between us.

I don't dare to say that out loud.

Nearly scared to even think it.

Sebastian's looking at me lovingly.

And I'm looking right back.

This may have started as a silly crush, but it has quickly grown into so much more.

We make our way to my coach, and Sebastian tells me about the articles about us.

I feel my heart hammering as he shows me the pictures.

We look like any other couple out enjoying their Sunday in London.

Part of me is angry that our moment is splattered across gossip sites.

It's not right.

Having private moments revealed to the whole world must be exhausting for a celebrity.

I know Luke isn't too happy about that part of his career, and it certainly created some challenges for him and Jessica early on in their relationship.

So far, they haven't been able to identify me since the pictures were taken from a distance and you can't really see my face.

Sebastian runs his knuckles down my face as he tells me that it's just a matter of time. Knowing the British press, they'll find out soon enough, and then my name will also be written right next to his.

"I'm sorry about this," he says, making me grab his hand.

"You have nothing to be sorry about. I'm sorry for you, having to deal with shit like this all the time."

It doesn't feel fair.

Guys like Sebastian and Luke never signed up for that kind of life.

They want to live out their athletic dreams.

Not grace the cover of every magazine.

"It's fine, Lily. I'm used to it. But they'll probably try to dig up all they can on you. When they find out you're the brother of Luke Hastings, they'll have plenty of fuel for their stories."

We settle into the couch, me lying with my back to his chest, our legs intertwined.

"I can handle it," I say.

"Can you, now, Lily?"

Sebastian runs his fingers over my boobs, making my nipples perk up at the contact.

I took off my bra earlier when I got back. Relaxation at home always calls for the most comfort.

It's nothing relaxing about the touches from Sebastian, though.

I turn around, placing my legs on either side of him as I press him down into the cushion.

I kiss him, groaning against his mouth when I feel his hard length against me.

"What do you think, Lily? Should we fuck in this apartment or the penthouse first?"

I'm going to burn up from his words alone.

"Here."

I drag my hands under his shirt, feeling his muscles before I move further down.

When I get to the waistband of his pants, he grabs my hands, stopping my movements.

Then he flips us around, leaving him on top.

"I was just getting to the good part," I murmur.

Sebastian chuckles before his hands continue their own exploration.

We're both eager to explore each other, fighting for contact as our tongues work together.

"Clothes off," he says, sitting back and dragging off his own sweater.

I lay there watching him, which makes him take matters into his own hands, not happy with my strip tempo.

He stands up and drags my pants off, which makes me laugh.

"Eager are we?" I tease him, enjoying the show as he pushes down his own pants. When he takes his boxers with them, leaving him completely naked, I'm the one who feels the need to speed things up.

Fuck, he's perfect.

I grab my top, take it off and toss it to the floor. Sebastian leans down, his hand going around my backside, before he lifts me.

I wrap my legs around his back, loving the feeling of my bare chest against his.

I'm happy to have my thong still, considering I would spread my wetness across his stomach from my arousal.

Something tells me he wouldn't mind.

"Yes, I'm dying to be inside you."

I lean down and kiss him as he carries me to the bedroom.

He puts me down, lying on top of me, before his fingers go inside my thong.

"Fucking perfect," he husks before he starts fucking me with two of his fingers.

I tear at his shoulders, dragging my nails down his arms, leaving marks in their way.

Sebastian watches me, and when he leans down, taking one of my nipples into his mouth whilst still working his fingers in my cunt and watching my face, I feel myself nearing the edge.

He sucks and nips at my nipple before he gives the same treatment to my other breast.

"Sebastian," I moan, falling apart as he rides out my orgasm.

When my breathing calms, Sebastian asks me about a condom.

I tell him they're in the bedside table, which he raises his eyebrows at.

"Been planning this, babe?"

His smile is blinding as he opens the drawer.

"Fuck yes, I have, and there's more fun stuff in that drawer," I tell him, feeling my heart pound in my chest.

He leans further out to get a better look whilst I hold my breath.

My earlier, idiot partners felt threatened by toys in the bedroom. Never wanting to try anything new. I would bring up a suggestion, and they would make me feel stupid for even asking.

Sebastian is quickly proving just how wrong those men have been for me.

He lets out a breath when he sees the handcuffs, a vibrator, some lube, and even a butt plug.

I felt a little wild during one of my shopping sprees, and the vibrator has been put to good use.

Sebastian has had me so sexually frustrated over these last few weeks, leaving me to get the vibrator.

"We'll definitely have some fun with that, but for now, I'll fuck you, just by myself."

He winks at me as he opens the condom with his teeth.

Just by himself sounds perfect to me.

He lines himself up at my entrance, and we both watch mesmerised as he pushes into me.

He looks into my eyes.

"You okay?"

I answer by locking my legs harder around him, pushing him farther into me.

"Yes, please move," I beg.

Sebastian bites my nipple.

"Such a fucking brat, aren't you?"

He withdraws before slamming back into me, making me cry out from pleasure.

He sets the perfect pace, and I meet him halfway.

I grab his hair, pulling tightly as he lifts one of my legs, changing the angle and letting him go even deeper.

"Fuck, Sebastian. You feel so good," I moan, my other hand finding his ass as I push him against me.

He leans back, holding my hips as he continues thrusting into me, holding my ass steady.

"I need your lips. Come here."

He drags me up against him, still keeping up his pace as he kisses me.

When his fingers move between us, working my clit, I fall apart, screaming his name.

Sebastian follows close, cursing and groaning my name as he comes.

We fall back into the bed, both of us breathing heavy.

When his arm sneaks around my body, pulling me to him, I feel the emotion in my throat.

Shit.

This is intense in every way.

Being with someone who fits you so perfectly feels scary. It also feels fantastic.

I sigh, cuddling closer to him, laying my head on his chest as he kisses my hair.

"Like I said—fucking perfect," he says, making me smile.

I look up at him.

"You also called me a brat," I say, secretly loving it.

Something tells me that he loves setting me straight. I know I push his buttons, and I would love it if he brought out his dominant side in the bedroom.

"Yeah, I got carried away," he says, reading my expression.

"I liked it," I whisper quietly, feeling the need to hide.

Christ.

I shouldn't feel so exposed voicing my desires, but . every time I've done it in the past, the guys have shut me out, leaving me with a hollow feeling inside.

Sebastian shifts our position, laying me across his body like a blanket.

"I get the feeling you've had some assholes in your bed, Lily, and even though I'll feel murderous, I do think I need to know."

On top of being a football and sex god, he seems to have the ability to read my mind as well.

I bite my lip, not really knowing where to start this.

"I guess it boils down to my personality. As you know, I like to flirt and not take myself too seriously. That goes in the bedroom as well. I've been with some men—or rather boys, I would call them—who've made me feel ashamed of asking for something," I tell him.

Sebastian is lazily running his fingers up and down my body, soothing me as he listens.

"Asking for what?" he asks, placing a lock of hair behind my ear.

Now, we get to the sex part, and where I've been met with discomfort before, Sebastian looks intrigued.

"Oral sex, for one," I tell him, which makes him roll his eyes. Sebastian has already redeemed my every oral sex experience when he ate me out like a starved man yesterday.

"Yeah, assholes, alright. Anything else?"

I cast my eyes down, the intensity of his gaze unwavering. He gently places his fingers under my chin, lifting my eyes back to him.

"Don't hide, Lily. If it gets too much, we'll stop, but we're doing this together. I'll tell you some of my kinks as well."

He winks at me, elevating the mood.

"I want to be dominated," I say, my voice small.

The need to run is real.

Sebastian's hold on me tightens, probably sensing my fears.

"That can definitely be arranged. What elements turn you on?"

Sebastian starts kissing down my throat, distracting me with his touch as I lay it all out on him.

A clever man this one.

Speaking about it feels intimidating, daunting.

When he starts kissing, nibbling, and touching me, it gets a little easier as my mind also enjoys the feel of him.

"Spanking. Bondage. Degradation."

The last part is one I've never dared voice to anyone. Never felt safe enough to do it. Sebastian is different, though. He doesn't make me feel bad or ashamed for wanting these things.

Sebastian surprises me when he slaps my ass—getting straight to work.

"You liked it then, when I called you a brat?" he asks against my lips.

"Yeah."

He flips us over and presses his hard cock against my thigh.

"I feel like the luckiest man alive," he murmurs against my skin

Sebastian leans down to my ear, raising goosebumps from the passion of the moment.

"And now, I'm going to fuck you so good, you'll fucking wish you never opened those legs for anyone else than me."

When Sebastian grabs a new condom and pushes into me, the last thing on my mind is the men before him.

Chapter 27

Sebastian

I lie there, gazing at Lily as she sleeps soundly beside me.

I've developed a kink of watching her sleep as well. I realise I've spent a fair share of time doing that since she got to London.

On the plane. When she fell asleep watching a movie. When she was sick. And now, after we've spent the night exploring each other's bodies.

It feels like a lot more than sex.

I feel like I've looked into her soul tonight, her raw fears and vulnerabilities as she told me about her douchebag partners and how they made her feel.

Just thinking about it makes me furious.

I bring her closer to me, letting her presence calm me.

I wasn't joking when I told her she's perfect.

I've always looked at her as this vibrant person no one can mess with or hurt.

Tonight, I got to see layers of her.

Of course she gets hurt. She's just better at hiding it.

I'm happy that she didn't hide from me. It took courage for her to open up, and I plan to treasure what she told me.

I was scared I went too far, calling her a brat in the heat of the moment.

Our banter is always playful, flirty.

Bringing it into the bedroom and elevating it could backfire on me.

She likes to mess with me, push me. I'd want nothing more than to set her straight sometimes.

When she told me she liked it, I knew we were perfect for each other.

I didn't doubt it, but you can never know.

Some people prefer vanilla sex, and that's fine. Everyone is entitled to do whatever they want.

Knowing that Lily is like me, though? That's fucking fantastic.

We've already put those toys of hers to good use.

I handcuffed her to the bed earlier, her legs spread wide as I fucked her from behind and used the vibrator on her.

She told me she had used the vibrator thinking about me these last weeks.

The vulnerability was there as she said it, but I reassured her that I was right there with her, getting myself off to the thought of her every morning in the shower.

I breathe in her scent, feeling my body relax in her presence.

I've wanted this woman for so long, I almost can't believe that I have her in my arms.

Knowing her brother also knows has lifted the heavy weight I've been carrying ever since she came to London.

Before she came here, I was able to contain my attraction to her, as I didn't see her as often as I'd like.

When she boarded that plane, everything was intensified.

It's been like heaven and hell all at once.

Having her close, lifting my spirits, and exploring the city with her.

Not being able to pull her as close as I'd really like, though, that has been tough.

I snuggle closer to her, enjoying the feeling of finally having her right where I've wanted for so long.

~

I'm walking hand in hand with Lily, enjoying the afternoon after we've spent most of the day in bed.

Sex or not, she still wants to explore the sights London has to offer and forces us to get some fresh air after spending hours wrapped up in each other.

I'm telling her about a dreadful photoshoot we did the day she got sick.

It involved too much nakedness and fruits in places they really have no business being, and we're both laughing hysterically.

"I thought we were done sexualising people for commercial use like that," Lily says before making me promise to bring her a copy when the photos drop.

When we turn a corner, I stop us in our tracks, holding Lily's hand firmly in my own.

Ashley is looking right at us.

I instinctively step in front of Lily, still holding her hand and making sure she's alright.

"Sebastian! I've been looking for you."

Ashley says it like she's a relative speaking to a family member, when in reality, she's someone I spent a maximum of ten minutes with, in a crowded, noisy club.

"You can stop looking for me and leave me alone," I say, my tone stern.

I'm done with this.

I've tried everything.

Letting her down gently.

Ignoring her.

It's time for her to let this go, because this is way out of line.

"Don't say that. I saw the articles and had to see her for myself. Can't believe you replaced me with her."

Oh, fuck no.

She did not.

"First of all, the only reason I ever looked your way is that you resembled her, and I was going crazy about my feelings for her. Secondly, that was the biggest fucking mistake I made as you could never be her."

I'm seething as I look down at her, and Ashley seems to understand that whatever she thought was between us was never there.

I was trying to forget about the woman who is holding me steady with her sole presence in this moment.

Lily steps forward, her chin raised as she looks at Ashley.

"You heard my man. Now, get lost before I call the police and have a restraining order imposed."

Ashley looks between us, clearly not pleased with what she's seeing, but the message registers loud and clear as she turns around and gets out of our way.

I'm hoping that will be the last time we ever see her.

"You okay?" I ask Lily, rubbing my hands up and down her arms. A habit I seem to have whenever my own nerves rise.

Touching her comforts me.

"Of course. Are you?"

I smile at her.

"Your man is very well," I say, my tone teasing as we both break out in smiles.

"You're sexy when you get possessive," I whisper in her ear.

"And you're sexy when you tell another woman she could never be me."

It might not have been the wisest thing to say, as I don't know how Ashley will react. I'm hoping she'll realise she never stood a chance.

"It's the truth," I say, and the breathtaking smile Lily aims my way makes my heart skip.

Yeah, no one could ever be her.

~

With Lily's hand in my own, we make our way out of the airport. We are heading towards the exit where we'll catch a taxi to our hotel.

When we round the corner, we're met with a loud "Surprise!" from Luke and Jessica, who are waiting for us in the arrivals hall.

Luke is wearing a cap and sunglasses, probably trying to hide his identity in the busy airport. His face is probably plastered all over the city, given the excitement over the potential world title being won this weekend.

Jessica is holding a neon pink banner that reads "Pick-up for the lovebirds" and it sends us both into laughter.

Having the conversation with Luke before this weekend turned out to be the best decision. If not, I wouldn't be able to cradle Lily's hand in my own, just like now.

Lily told me that Jessica was her wing-woman back in Australia, trying to get my attention.

Lily had all of my attention long before that, and seeing her that evening nearly sent me over the edge, but Luke interrupted us when I was sure I was going to cross that line for the first time.

Seeing Jessica's excitement about us warms my heart, and the smile Luke is sending my way reassures me that he's okay with this.

He's told me so himself, but those worries don't disappear overnight.

When we reach them, hugs are exchanged, and Jessica is still beaming at us like she's won the lottery.

"Happiness suits you, man," Luke says as he gives me a hug.

The girls are already giggling at something, probably eager to get rid of us to have their girl time.

"Thanks, Luke," I say, feeling the emotion thick in my throat.

I've been Luke's own relationship guru whenever he's had challenges with Jessica, and knowing I got his support now means a lot.

We make our way out of the airport, the girls going ahead in their own bubble.

I bet Lily is happy to be back in the States for a few days and for the opportunity to catch up with Jessica.

She has her FaceTime calls, but I know for myself that it's not the same as the real deal.

"Ready to be crowned the new champion?" I ask Luke, knowing the most important weekend of his career is ahead.

"Yeah, and now that everyone is showing up, this title has to be mine," he says.

His whole family is here for the weekend, but Luke seems content and relaxed.

What will be, will be.

~

"You athletes and your egos, my girls are struggling," Lily says as she finishes telling Luke and Jessica about her friends and their challenges with their athletes in the assignment they're doing.

"Not everyone," I comment, giving her a knowing look, and looking over to Luke.

Two of the men in her life are athletes after all.

"Especially you two," Jessica cuts in, causing the girls to snicker.

I'm eager to squeeze Lily's waist, but I'm still getting used to being affectionate with her with Luke around.

He's been nothing but supportive, but I don't think he would appreciate me groping his sister in front of him.

I can tell Lily would like me to touch her more affectionately though as she obliviously doesn't care about having her brother around.

Teasing her and keeping her on edge may be a little satisfying, knowing the tension will make it that much sweeter when we're alone later today.

We finish our lunch, and Luke is off with Jessica to the pre-race spectacle and their media duties.

When they leave, Lily seems eager for some alone time, just like me.

She brings her arms around my neck and gives me a quick kiss.

"I didn't know you were this scared of my dear brother, Sebastian. Where is the man who gave me a very public orgasm under a table?" she says with a teasing glint in her eyes.

I pinch her ass before leaning down to her ear.

"Such a fucking brat, aren't you? Someone has to behave," I say, pulling her closer to me.

My words ignite the fire in her eyes, knowing she likes it when I push back.

I lean down and bring my lips to hers, giving her a proper kiss this time.

Just as I've grabbed a hold of her ass and Lily's pressing her body closely to mine, I hear someone clear their throat.

We break apart, our arms still around each other.

"Will probably never get used to this part of your relationship. Christ, we've gone for one minute and you're already going at it," Luke says, picking up his wallet, which he obviously forgot.

Now, Lily is the one blushing.

"Sorry, man. We'll try to tone it down around you," I say, scratching my neck.

I don't know if I'll be able to keep that promise, but I'll try for my best friend.

"It's fine, just new," he says before he's on his way again.

Lily rests her head against my chest, groaning out loud.

"Gosh, how embarrassing that was."

I chuckle at her.

I mean, sure, it's embarrassing having him catch us like that, but the bigger part of me is so relieved of having

Luke know about my feelings for her, that the awkwardness is all worth it.

I'd rather have that than having to hide any longer.

For Lily, though, it may be more awkward, considering I'm her brother's best friend. I know Luke's teased her growing up about having a crush on me.

"At least we were wearing clothes," I say, making Lily push at my chest and roll her eyes.

"Yeah, I think the public sex should be kept at bay considering all the media and photographers," she says.

She's right, but the temptation is definitely there, knowing how much she liked it the last time.

"Yeah, we'll save that for London," I say, feeling a weight in my stomach.

When we travel back to the UK, Lily doesn't have much time left before she's going back to the US, this time for good.

This is all so new, and even though I don't want to stress too much about this, I know that, at least for me, I'm not looking forward to her going back.

I also don't want to stand in her way or hold her back from anything she wants to do.

What am I supposed to say to her?

I want you to continue your life in London with me, making me breakfast and going to the stadium with me.

Having dinner with Harriet. Cheer for me, wearing your jerseys, and go back home together afterward.

I know that life would bore Lily. She likes adventures, travelling, and exploring new things, and I'm afraid that a life with me in London wouldn't be enough for her.

I couldn't live with myself if that were the case, and she gave up her dreams for me.

So for now, that weight is pushed as far down as possible, whilst I tell myself to enjoy the time we still have.

Chapter 28

Lily

I have my arms around Jessica, squeezing her as my life depends on it, as Luke is finishing the last lap of the Las Vegas Grand Prix.

Just a few more turns, and he'll be the new world champion.

A childhood dream is becoming a reality.

When he crosses the finish line, fireworks erupt into the sky, and the cheers in the BMW garage go crazy.

Half of the engineers are hanging on the barricades, cheering Luke on as he crosses the line.

The tears streaming down my cheeks match Jessica's, who is an even bigger mess than I am.

"He did it," she whispers, the pride in her eyes evident before we exchange another hug.

Then the whole family exchanges embraces, emotions running high.

I'm grateful we're able to experience this together, being here on the most important day in Luke's career.

He's worked for this moment his whole life, and now it's here.

I watch the screens as Luke takes a victory lap around the track, waving to the fans and soaking up the atmosphere.

I feel Sebastian's arms around my stomach before he lays his head on my shoulder as I lean back into him.

"Can you believe it?" I ask, pride swelling in my chest at seeing Luke and the support he's receiving.

He's been the golden boy, the one everyone expected to win this whole season.

But Formula 1 is filled with rivalry and unpredictable turns at every corner.

You never know what can happen.

He's had his challenges, but he pushed through and proved himself once and for all.

"Yeah," Sebastian murmurs in my ear, and when I turn to look at him, I see the emotion in his eyes as well.

"Sebby, are you crying?" I ask, unable to contain my teasing.

He scoffs and mutters an "of course not", but his smile tells me otherwise.

He knows he's full of shit.

Sebastian has known Luke almost as long as I have; they've been there for each other their whole life.

No wonder he's feeling emotional, just like the rest of us.

"It's okay. I won't tell anyone that you're a cry-baby," I tell him, and when he nips at my earlobe, the desire surges inside of me.

Just the reaction I wanted.

I might enjoy teasing him, knowing he'll put me in my place later.

"Careful," he whispers, making me smile.

Luke has finally parked his car, and we make our way over to where the rest of the team has gathered.

Luke stands on top of his car, cheering with his arms over his head and looking up at the sky.

Then he runs over to his team, who catch him and engulf him in hugs and more pats on the back than you can count.

When he spots Jessica in the crowd, he runs straight to her, lifting her up into his arms as she places her hands on his helmet and kisses the part covering his mouth.

Cue the tears again.

This title means a lot to Luke, but having Jessica by his side through it all—and being able to celebrate it together with her—might be the bigger victory for him.

Our parents have always been a little worried that he wouldn't find someone who loves him for who he is.

Not his name, money, or fame.

Then, he stumbled—quite literally—into Jessica on one of her first days here in the paddock.

She knew who he was, but she sure as hell didn't bow to the golden boy.

No wonder we also became fast friends.

"Will that be us when I win the Champions League?" Sebastian asks me.

He also admires Luke and Jessica and their moment together.

The butterflies in my stomach go crazy.

I would love for that to be us.

And the fact that Sebastian just said that suggests he considers us long-term.

He hasn't said or done anything to imply otherwise, but part of me has been a little worried about what will happen when I go back to the States.

Will we do long-distance?

How will that go?

I've gotten so used to having him around, I know I'll miss him dearly.

I know what I want, but I'm not sure if he wants the same thing.

Being in London has been amazing, and not just because of Sebastian, even though he's a big part of it.

I love the city and its atmosphere.

I've always wanted to travel and try to live somewhere else, but life hasn't taken me down that route before my London adventure began.

Now, I don't want it to end.

I want to continue living there and explore all the sights I haven't seen. Try the foods I haven't yet.

I'm scared to take that up with the man behind me.

What if he wants to go back to his routine without me?

I'm sure he would make sure the blow was as soft as possible, but I'm terrified to find out.

So for now, I relish in the feeling of knowing he at least sees this as something more long-term, no matter the format.

~

I apply the last of my makeup, a smile taking over my face.

I look good if I can say so myself.

We're getting ready to head out and celebrate.

Being in Vegas means I had the opportunity to take it all out in the makeup, hair, and clothing department, which I love.

Nothing like having the opportunity to pull out the big guns.

My hair is curled, my eyes are smoky, and my outfit is daring.

The skirt I'm wearing is tight around my hips, and I've paired it with a top that reaches my throat, but almost my entire back is exposed.

Family around and all that.

Better to have the back exposed than the girls in front.

I'm eager to see Sebastian's reaction as well.

I kicked him out of the bathroom as soon as he finished his shower.

As I turn the door handle, I'm the first one to stare.

Sebastian is facing the mirror in our room, his back to me, but I see his reflection in the mirror.

His shirt is open, exposing his abs as he's pulling at the tie hanging around his neck.

When he catches my eye in the mirror, he halts his movements before he turns around, taking me in.

He traces every curve of my body with his eyes, taking his time admiring me.

When he reaches my face and eyes, he gives me a sinful smile.

"Come over here, Lily," he commands.

I'm usually very comfortable in high heels, but now, with the desire simmering between us and the anticipation of what he'll do, I'm a little unsteady as I make my way over to him.

When I reach him, he lifts his hand and lightly runs his fingers from my cheek, down behind my neck, and over my exposed back.

"Magnificent," he whispers.

Christ.

Is it possible to come just from the sound of a voice?

I might have to put that theory to the test.

Just as I'm about to open my mouth, he puts two of his fingers inside my mouth before he lifts a single eyebrow.

"Suck," he orders.

I do as he tells me, taking my time running my tongue around his fingers and looking into his eyes.

Ever since our first night together, he's proved just how wrong the men before him were for me.

Sebastian gets me.

He understands my needs and desires.

And he'll make sure I enjoy every second of it.

He withdraws his fingers before he tells me to bend over and hold on to the mirror.

"I can recall some comments, Lily, can you?" he says, his hand slowly caressing my ass.

"Hmmm, no. I can't," I say, and when his hand comes down on my ass, I cry out from the sting and the pleasure.

He takes hold of my skirt, lifting it up over my ass, exposing my thong.

"You sure?" he asks.

I'm looking at him in the mirror, watching him as he stands behind me.

"Yeah, I think you need to remind me," I say, eager for him to continue.

His hand comes down again, and I grip the mirror harder in my hands, trying to steady myself.

"I can recall you being a fucking brat—calling me a cry-baby, for instance," he says, slapping my ass once more.

I moan, feeling the wetness gather in my thong as Sebastian runs his hand down from my ass to my thighs.

He doesn't touch me where I need him the most, taking his time and dragging out my pleasure.

"And then there was something about being scared of your brother."

Another slap, and I can feel the heat rising on my butt cheeks.

Sebastian goes down to his knees directly behind me, and even though I feel slightly exposed, I trust him to make me feel good.

He drags his finger all the way from my calf up the inside of my leg, before I'm certain he'll finally touch me where I need him.

But then, he makes his way down again, taking his sweet time as I buckle against him, desperate for his touch.

"What do you want, Lily?" he asks, his hands moving slowly.

"You," I say, feeling like I might die if he doesn't touch me soon.

"Finally, a correct answer," he says before rewarding me. He plunges two of his fingers inside me, and I cry out, meeting his thrust as he finds the perfect rhythm.

"Look at you, fucking my fingers like you've been made for it," he says, and when I look up into the mirror, our eyes meet, the intensity overwhelming as he pleasures my body.

"Sebastian," I moan, the sensations taking over.

Just as I think I can't hold back any longer, he drags some of my wetness up toward my butthole. He watches me in the mirror, looking for any signs of discomfort or that I don't want this.

I've never gone down that route before, but I'm quickly learning that anything Sebastian does to my body makes me feel fantastic, so I trust him to do this as well.

I give him a nod before he continues smearing my wetness, making sure I'm slick.

Then he slowly sinks his finger inside my hole, telling me to relax.

The sensation is new, foreign, but as I get used to his touch and he continues fingering me, the pleasure starts building again.

"How are you feeling, Lily?" he asks me, watching me intently in the mirror.

"So fucking good," I say, breathless from the pleasure.

As he intensifies the pressure and starts circling my clit at the same time, I feel the orgasm building in my core.

"Sebastian, I'm close," I moan.

He continues his movements, taking my body to heights it's never experienced before.

The orgasm rocks my body, and one of my hands slips from the mirror, but Sebastian quickly catches me, still pleasuring me and riding out the orgasm as my body turns to mush.

Fucking hell.

That was intense.

Sebastian gathers me in his arms before he puts me on the bed.

"Good?" he asks, a twinkle in his eyes.

He almost looks as drunk on pleasure as me.

"Fantastic," I tell him, bringing his head down for a kiss.

He settles over me, and even though we're still clothed—or at least partly—I've never felt closer to him.

"Christ, I didn't plan for this, but you coming out of that bathroom looking like you did… I couldn't control myself," he says.

My own hands start exploring his body, my arms going inside his open shirt before I caress the muscles in his back. Then I make my way to his front and down toward his crotch.

"What do you want, Sebastian? My mouth or my cunt?" I whisper before I bring my hand inside his trousers.

When I grab a hold of his cock, he's already hard and aching.

"Cunt," he says, before he pushes his pants down over his ass.

Not getting completely naked seems to be the norm for us, but I love it.

I open my legs as Sebastian lines up his cock at my entrance. He simply pushes my thong to the side before pushing inside me.

We both groan out in pleasure.

"Fuck, Sebastian."

"Yeah, that's what we're doing."

He smirks down at me, making me roll my eyes at him.

Christ, he even brings out our banter in bed.

He leans down, taking a nipple into his mouth before biting down, causing me to arch my back.

Sebastian grabs a hold of my hips, leaning slightly back as he ups his pace.

I bring my hands up over my head, pushing against the headboard as he continues fucking me.

"Lily, you feel amazing."

He thrusts harder into me, and I meet him halfway.

His grip on me turns punishing, and a part of me hopes he'll leave marks.

I'd love to have a memory of this evening.

"I told myself I would spare your face, considering the makeup, but fuck, Lily, I need you," he says before his arms go around my back, lifting me up towards his own face, before his lips come down on my own.

He continues fucking me, our tongues twisting in open-mouth kisses.

I couldn't care less for the makeup.

I'll do it again.

The new position causes his cock to rub against my clit, and I scream as I come.

Sebastian follows closely after, holding me tight in his arms as he spills into me.

It takes me a moment to register that we just fucked without a condom.

Sebastian seems oblivious as he lies down in the bed, taking me with him in his arms.

I'm not worried, considering I'm on the pill and clean.

I've never been so caught up in pleasure that I've even considered it.

"Sebastian," I murmur.

We're breathing heavy, and I wonder just how much time we've spent. We'll probably be a little late to the party, but oh well.

"Yeah?"

"We didn't use a condom," I say, and he sits up quickly in bed, looking down at me.

"Shit, I'm so sorry, Lily. I'm clean, and you make me fucking crazy, so I didn't even think about it. Fuck, I'm sorry."

His panic is slightly adorable, and I decide to toy with him a little.

"Okay. I hope you're ready to be a father, considering I'm on no birth control and should be in my fertile window."

If his panic was bad before, it's terrifying now.

But then his expression calms, and he smiles softly as he looks at my stomach.

"If that's the case, we'll figure it out."

Now I'm the one panicking.

He can't be serious.

I'm not ready to be a mother.

I was just joking.

He can't be serious, can he?

Amid his statement, I even forget that I'm on freaking birth control.

"Ehm, I was just jok—"

Sebastian bursts out laughing.

When he calms down, he gives me a look.

"I know you're on birth control, babe. It's true that we'd make it work even if you did become pregnant, but when you decide to mess with me, I have to get you back sometimes," he says, so pleased with himself.

I guess I deserved that.

He gives me a quick peck before taking my hand and dragging me out of bed.

"Come on. Let's fix our freshly fucked look before we meet up with the family."

~

We're in a crowded club, the music flowing from the speakers as the flickering lights match the rhythm of the song. I'm sitting in a booth together with Jessica. The boys are somewhere else, probably getting hammered.

Everyone's been eager to treat Luke to anything he wants this evening.

Sebastian told me he would stay low on the alcohol, but you can never know.

"So, tell me everything. How long did it take for Sebastian to make a move?" Jessica asks me.

We haven't had too much time to really catch up ever since we got to Vegas, as she and Luke have been busy with their jobs.

Now, though, we finally have some much-needed girl time.

"Gosh, too long. I had to pull out some tricks," I tell her, thinking back to the game night at his apartment and my obvious flirting with his teammates.

That night definitely changed things between us.

There had been moments prior to that, but I pushed him that evening.

I tell Jessica about my time in London and all the things I've experienced with Sebastian.

Our breakfast, movie nights, his family visiting and the overall fun we've had thus far.

When I'm done, I let out a huge sigh, contemplating how life will be when I go back to Seattle.

"You don't want to leave, do you?" Jessica asks me with a gentle smile.

"No, I don't. But I'm scared to bring it up. I'm not used to feeling too vulnerable in a relationship with a man. Everything is different with him," I tell her honestly.

The thought of not having a label on a relationship hasn't been something I've cared too much about before.

Now, I'm anxious for us to make this exclusive so I can lessen my worries.

It's not like I think Sebastian would be with anyone else, but insecurities I've never really dealt with before have appeared.

When I started the London adventure, I always expected to be excited to go back home, take the trip with my girls, and get back to my routine.

Now, that all feels like the last thing I want to do.

"I think you should just talk to him, Lily. Communication and trust are everything you need. Trust me, I know."

I know she's right, but it doesn't make it less daunting.

"Besides, Sebastian looks at you like you're his whole world. You have nothing to worry about," she says, squeezing my hand in her own.

I look over to where the boys are playing darts, immediately catching Sebastian's eyes on my own before he winks at me.

He sure feels like my whole world when he lights me up with a simple look across the room.

Chapter 29

Sebastian

We're enjoying an early-morning breakfast before Lily and I travel to the airport and back to London.

We stayed out late last night, celebrating Luke and his title, but I didn't drink much alcohol, which I'm grateful for now.

Can't say the same for my best friend, who's sporting a real bad hangover.

I'm surprised he even made it to breakfast with us, but Jessica insisted they spent some time with us before we left—and what Jessica says goes.

Luke is down bad for his girl, but I can't really say too much about it, considering my own feelings and inability to say no to Lily.

"God, I'm never drinking again. This hangover might kill me," Luke groans into his hands.

We all chuckle around the table, Jessica laying a comforting hand on his back.

"Yeah, they didn't hold back on you," she says, referencing all the drinks that were treated his way yesterday.

It was practically a line of people in his team wanting to treat the newly crowned champion, myself included.

"Stop being a baby," Lily says, happy to tease her brother about his misery.

Our food arrives, and even though the meal is nice, I'm looking forward to going back to the city and having our breakfast routine back.

Lily cooks a stellar breakfast, and it's even better now that I get to wake up with her by my side before we start our day.

"On a serious note, Luke, we're all very proud of you," Lily says a while later when we've talked about the way that led Luke to his victory.

He's had tough competition and challenges thrown his way, but he pushed through.

"Thanks, sis. I'm glad you made the trip—both of you," he says, looking over to me as well.

Even though our trip was short, it was well worth it. I'm happy that we were able to be here for such a monumental moment in his career.

~

"Feeling alright?" I ask Lily, who sits in the seat next to me.

We've been flying for about an hour, and we'll land in the middle of the night. Then I'll have practice, which will be tough, but I'll manage.

"Yeah. I'm excited to go back to London," she says, and I see my opening.

I've been wanting to talk to her about her project coming to an end and how we'll move forward.

"You have two weeks left?" I ask, feeling stupid for even asking.

I know how many days she has; I'm dreading the countdown of our time together.

"Yes, then I'll go back, and then the trip to the Caribbean, if we make it there."

This is news to me.

Trip to the Caribbean?

"You going away?" I ask, trying to keep my tone as nonchalant as possible.

I guess a small part of me was hoping she might stay a little longer, given the changes in our relationship, but again, I don't want to stand in the way of what she loves.

"Yeah, the girls from college and I have been planning a trip, but Mira and Kait are still struggling, so we'll likely have to wing it."

This really shouldn't be surprising.

I know Lily loves to travel.

No wonder she'd like to travel after spending weeks in gloomy London.

That doesn't stop the feeling of dread that settles in my stomach: the realization that I might not see her for several weeks—hell, maybe months.

"That sounds fantastic," I say, even though the words feel like sandpaper rubbing against my throat.

"Yeah, I guess," she says, looking lost in thought as she looks away from me and out of the window.

The silence stretches between us before Lily mutters something about getting some sleep.

As she wanders off to the bedroom in the back of the jet, I'm lost in thought.

It will be fine.

She'll be gone for a few weeks and will hopefully come visit me after.

This is the part of my job that is hard. Taking trips, especially across the pond, isn't the easiest.

My schedule simply doesn't allow for much travel during the season.

That leaves the people in my life as the ones who visit me most of the time.

Will Lily be okay with that?

I guess I won't know if I don't ask her.

I was planning to do so, but then the trip to the Caribbean was mentioned, and I realised she may be eager to get back to her life in the States: her friends, school, and family.

Nevertheless, I plan on enjoying the rest of our time together, and we'll handle the rest when the time comes.

~

I'm counting down the minutes until practice ends, and I'll get to go back to my apartment.

The tiredness is kicking my ass, making each metre heavier than the last as I run.

Playing midfield has never felt this tough.

"Good trip to Vegas?" Dean snickers beside me, enjoying my obvious misery.

"Yeah, the lack of sleep is killing me."

Usually, I would host game night tonight, but I told the guys I wasn't up for it after my trip.

They'll come over someday later this week instead when I'm all rested and back in shape.

I do look forward to having Lily for myself for the evening.

The last few days have been a lot of socializing, and although it's been a good time, I'm eager to be just the two of us for the night.

Practice finally ends, and I grab a quick shower before heading home.

When I get to my apartment, I'm confused when I don't find Lily there.

She slept over when we got back, and I expected to find her here.

I don't see any messages from her, so I decide to just head down and see if she's in her own apartment.

I should probably terminate the lease so she'll have to stay with me for these last twelve days.

Yes, I'm counting.

I take the elevator down to her floor and don't bother knocking. As usual, her door is unlocked, and I walk right in.

Lily is seated on a barstool, working on her assignment.

When she spots me, she looks up, but quickly goes back to the notes in front of her.

"Hey, babe. Are you busy? Why are you down here?" I ask her, confused about why she'd work down here instead of my flat.

She writes down something, her eyes still cast downward, and I feel my frustrations growing.

Why won't she look at me?

Have I done something wrong?

"I just thought you'd appreciate some space. I've been at your apartment, your jet, and the hotel room in Vegas."

I sense the vulnerability in her voice, wondering why she'd get that impression.

"Do you want space from me?" I ask, moving closer to her.

She finally looks up and lets out a breath.

"No, I don't, and that's scaring me," she says, her voice barely a whisper at the end.

I stand in front of her before I lean down and press my lips against hers.

Pouring all my longing, wants, and love for this woman into it.

"I don't want any space either, Lily. I was disappointed when I didn't find you in the apartment when I got back, so please, just come home with me?" I plead with her.

This may be a simple request to take the elevator back up together for the evening, but to me, it means so much more—even if I'm not able to tell her that just yet.

"Yeah, I'd like that," she says, pressing her lips against mine again.

I bring my arms around her, dragging her up against my body.

I set her down on the counter before I start kissing down her neck and chest, hungry to have her as close as possible.

"Eager, Bennet?" she teases, her own hands exploring my body as I sink down in front of her.

"Fucking starved, babe," I tell her, pulling her pants down her legs.

I lick the inside of her leg, and Lily grabs a hold of my hair as she leans her head back, a moan escaping her.

"Be a good girl and spread those legs."

She obeys, and I take a moment to drink her in.

She's only wearing a tight top and a deep green thong, but it's her face that really draws me in.

The smile she gives me, the confidence shining off of her—it's all fucking perfect.

I hold eye contact as I lower down to her heat, a simple swipe of my tongue on the outside of her thong.

"Sebastian."

My name is a plea on her lips.

I run my fingers up the inside of her legs, enjoying the feel of her smooth skin beneath my own.

"What, babe?"

"Please do something."

She doesn't have to ask me twice.

I pull at her thong, dragging it off her, before I lay my hands on top of her thighs and press my tongue against her heat.

She buckles under me, lying herself back on the counter, her hand still in my hair, gripping and pulling as I continue fucking her with my tongue.

I add a finger, driving her towards the edge.

When she comes, she moans my name as I ride out her orgasm, feeling drunk on her taste.

When her breathing calms, I stand up and lean down over her before I give her a kiss.

"Fucking perfect," I tell her.

Some may not be too keen on kissing when your partner's just gone down on you, but Lily doesn't mind.

As our kissing turns heated, her hand travels between us, inside my pants, where she grabs a hold of my cock.

I'm hard and ready, and Lily seems to enjoy the weight of me in her hands as she starts jerking me off.

"You feel so good," she says.

I pull down my pants, both of us looking at her hand working my cock so good.

I groan out loud, and when I feel the pressure start building, I grab her hand.

"Take off your top, Lily. I want you completely naked," I tell her, kicking off my pants before grabbing my shirt and pulling it off.

She does the same before I grab her legs and pull her to the edge of the counter.

"Are you ready, baby?"

"Always."

I push inside her in a hard thrust, both of us moaning in pleasure.

We fit together so perfectly.

"Fuck, Sebastian."

Her desperation matches my own as we climb each other's bodies, trying to get as close as possible.

Tongues twisting in open-mouthed kisses.

Hands roaming across all the skin we can reach.

"Fucking mine," I tell her, looking into her eyes, desperate for her to meet me halfway.

She does—every time.

"Yours," she confirms.

I play with her clit, sending her over the edge with me following closely after.

When we've caught our breath, I kiss her deeply, humming as I press my chest against her.

I can tell Lily has something on her mind, the uncertainty evident in her eyes as she gazes up at me.

"What is it?" I ask her, running a hand down her cheek.

"Did you mean it? That I'm yours? Or was it the heat of the moment? It's okay if it was, I just want to know."

Lily never stops surprising me.

In my mind, she's been mine from the moment I told my fucking teammates to lay off her.

"Christ, I'm lying on top of you with my cock still inside you. Of course you're mine, Lily."

Her smile is breathtaking, the relief evident in her face.

"Come on—let's take a shower, and I'll show you once more just how mine you are."

"I'd love that."

~

We've just finished dinner together with Harriet when Lily gets a call and excuses herself quickly.

I know she hasn't been able to catch up with her girls since we got back a couple of days ago.

As Lily leaves the room, I start helping Harriet clean up the kitchen.

"I'm sad that she's leaving soon. It's been nice having a woman around here as well. No offence," Harriet says.

Just like me, she's dreading the take-off back to America, which is approaching faster than I'd like.

"Yeah, none taken. I'll miss her as well," I tell her, looking down at my hands as I rinse off our plates.

Long-distance relationship.

Something I've never done.

I've never really done any type of relationship.

But with Lily, I'll take whatever I can get.

She's mine, and I'm hers; and for now, that's everything that matters.

"Do you think she would stay? If you asked?"

Harriet's not the first to think of this. I've thought about it several times, considering asking her to just stay, or come back to me as soon as she can.

It's been on the tip of my tongue, but then I remember her trip, and how she lights up whenever she mentions something new she'd like to try or a place to visit.

I don't want to be the reason she lost her spark, all because she was back in my condo, waiting for me to get back from practice to have dinner and movie nights.

That's my perfect dream.

But not hers.

"I don't know. Maybe, but she loves travelling, exploring new places, and socialising. I'm worried she'd be bored with this life."

We haven't been together for that long, so it feels like too much to even ask her to consider moving here with me—a whole different continent away from her family and friends.

"You don't know if you don't ask, Sebastian James."

My name never feels as long and serious as when Harriet says it with that tone.

"Yeah, I'll try," I say, giving her a wink, which makes her shake her head at me and mutter "men" under her breath.

Chapter 30

Lily

I settle into Sebastian's bed, happy to finally be able to catch up with the girls.

Each takes their turn telling us all the latest developments with their project.

Luckily, Mira is doing better with her team, and she's on her way back to schedule and ready for our trip.

She's been able to collect more data and should be ready to meet up at college as planned.

Wendy, like me, hasn't met too many challenges and is soon headed back from Brazil.

Then we have Kait and her dreaded sailor.

"I might just have to kick him overboard. Do you think I can change my project to be about stuck-up athletes who don't seem interested in improving their performance?"

She tells us that even though she's managed to collect a lot of data around the sport and how it works, the core of our assignment should be linked to the athlete or athletes we're researching.

It's too late for her to pick another sport.

So now, she's contemplating how she can find another sailor—preferably close by.

"I'll probably try to meet up with you later, hopefully in the Caribbean when the sailor is lost at sea for good."

We all chuckle at her dramatics.

Kait could never hurt anyone.

When it's time for me to catch them up, I'm feeling torn.

Part of me is excited for our trip and some well-needed time in the sun.

The other part of me is dreading leaving London, Sebastian, and the routine I've grown to love over the last month.

I feel better knowing we're exclusive and will do long-distance, but again, it just doesn't feel right.

"I actually went ahead and became the girlfriend of my athlete," I tell them, which sends the girls on the other end into hysterics.

Mira knows about my crush on Sebastian, but being the famous athlete he is, I never dared to tell the others.

Even though I hoped he felt the same as I did, the insecurities were there when I came here.

Therefore, I kept my crush a secret from most of my friends.

"Is that even allowed?" Wendy asks, and Mira rolls her eyes.

"It's not like she'll write that, 'he told me he performs best after we've fucked the night before' in her assignment."

I snort. Leave it to Mira to be blunt.

Before coming here, I had already decided to keep Sebastian anonymised in the final paper.

He's always been a good friend, and I would never want anyone to take advantage of the things he's told me.

"Will we get to meet this man any time soon?" Kait asks me.

"Honestly, I don't know. His life is here in London, and I'm still getting used to the thought of doing long-distance when we're practically living together now," I tell them.

"I'm sure you'll make it work," Wendy says.

We move on to other things and decide to book our tickets before they get too expensive. Kait will hopefully meet us there when she's sorted out the mess with her athlete.

It's a mix of excitement and dread I feel when we've hung up, and I look at my calendar.

When I go back to Seattle, I'll first be there for one week to meet with my supervisors.

Then, we'll leave for our trip, which we've set for around four weeks. We haven't booked our return flights, so the possibility of cutting it short is there, but I don't know how the girls would feel if I left them early for my man.

That means five whole weeks without Sebastian.

Gosh, I'm pathetic.

I've gone months—hell, years—with a crush on this man and managed just fine without seeing him for long.

Now, though, this is much more than a silly crush.

I sigh, contemplating how I'll leave this perfect bubble.

~

"Have you looked in my diary, Sebastian James?"

I rest my hands on my hips because this is starting to get ridiculous.

All week, Sebastian has "randomly" checked off several of the boxes on my London-adventure list.

When I look back, it's become quite obvious he knows of my list, considering all the things we've done together.

Now, I'm starting to get suspicious.

It's way too many coincidences for this to be random suggestions from him.

It all started with my trip to the cathedral, which he suggested we do together.

Our night out in the city when I got to sing my heart out on the dance floor.

I'm starting to think that the choice of club wasn't that accidental, and that he chose that, knowing I'd get to check off another point on my list.

Then, the trip to the Sky Garden, together with his family.

This week, though, he's ramped up the efforts, taking me to every single restaurant on my list—even taking a freaking London cab with me, although I know he prefers driving himself.

He gives me his most innocent smile.

"Maybe."

I'm touched by his actions, but for every checked mark, I'm reminded of how this is all coming to an end in a few short days.

I press down the emotion in my throat, overwhelmed by the feelings he evokes in me.

Not knowing what to say, I go straight into his arms, hugging him tightly as I feel my eyes watering.

Get a grip, Lily.

It's just a couple of weeks.

We'll be fine.

"Thank you."

I sniffle into his shirt, and Sebastian leans back, taking in my expression.

He rests his hands gently on my cheeks, wiping away the single tear that runs down.

"Baby, you deserve to see the whole world. The least I could do is show you London."

His words don't lessen the emotions inside me.

~

It's our last night together, and we're spending it in perfect Lily and Sebastian style: cuddled up on the couch after a wonderful dinner together with Harriet.

My flight is at noon tomorrow, and I'm trying to enjoy my time with Sebastian, but it all feels heavy because I don't know when I'll see him next.

"Babe, I really need for us to plan when we'll see each other next, because I feel like I might be sick from the feeling of saying goodbye tomorrow and not knowing."

I sit up on the couch, needing to have a plan.

Something I can cling to when it all gets too much.

"We've talked about this. You'll come back here when you get back from your trip with the girls," Sebastian says, putting a lock of hair behind my ear.

This is true.

We had planned that, but he told me he'll send a jet, so I don't have a ticket—which may be why I'm panicking.

Gosh.

I might be going crazy over this man.

It certainly feels that way.

That is still five weeks away, which right now feels like a lifetime.

"Lily, we'll be fine. It's just a couple of weeks. We'll talk every day," he soothes me.

He's made it clear that we'll handle this.

"Yeah, I know. I'm sorry for panicking. I'm just feeling emotional knowing we'll have to say goodbye tomorrow."

Sebastian pulls me on top of him, giving me a deep kiss.

"It's not goodbye, babe. It's a see you later."

I snort, but he brings out a smile on my face nevertheless.

"Yeah, a see you in five weeks later."

Chapter 31

Sebastian

The last couple of days have been hard. I tried to keep it together for the sake of Lily and me.

I could tell she's been struggling, but I didn't know how to help her properly.

I wanted to make our last week together special, checking off as many points on her lists as possible; but it also became a harsh reminder and a countdown until that flight left the terminal.

When she was lying in my arms, sad to say goodbye, I almost begged her to stay.

But then, I remembered the spark in her eyes when she told me about all the wonderful sights she's planning on exploring in the Caribbean.

Therefore, I had to be strong for both of us, making sure she boarded that plane—even though it felt like part of me flew away together with her.

It may be hard to say goodbye, but it would be even worse if she gave up everything for me.

I want her to live her life to the fullest, even if it means I'll only have her when her adventures lead her back to me.

I'll be here in my condo waiting with a romcom and a can of Coke for her.

~

Has it always been this quiet in my apartment?

Day four without Lily, and I'm realising just how dull and quiet my apartment is without her.

Just as I'm thinking about her, like I spend most of my time doing, her face lights up my phone with an incoming FaceTime call.

"Hey, beautiful."

I prop my phone up on the counter and see that she's walking, probably on campus.

"Hey, handsome. How is gloomy London?" she asks, and I feel myself relax as I talk with her.

Our calls have quickly become my favourite part of the day. She'll tell me about all the things she accomplished the day before and what she has planned for the day whilst I basically sit and admire her.

Then she'll ask me if I have anything exciting to tell her, and pout whenever I tell her that it's the same old.

I wake up, go to practice, eat lunch, have my meetings, another practice or workout, maybe a game.

Then, I'll head home, eager for her to call me when her day begins.

The same routine I've always had, but now, it leaves me feeling empty.

Therefore, I've promised myself to go do things I know Lily would enjoy.

A way for me to have her closer to me in a way.

When she asks me about my day, expecting me to say "same old", she lights up when I tell her that I actually went to the cathedral on the way back from the stadium.

"Really? That's great, Sebastian."

Her joy is contagious as she beams through the phone, and I might have to go do all the things on her lists just to see her reaction when I tell her about them.

"I really wanted to kiss you that day," I mutter, remembering how much I was struggling trying to contain my affection for her. I often find myself looking at the pictures she took of us.

"I really wanted you to kiss me that day. And any other day for that matter," she says, winking at me.

I'm glad she seems to be in good spirits, enjoying her time back at college.

This is what I wanted. For her to be happy.

She meets up with her friend, Mira, and we say our goodbyes.

The words are at the tip of my tongue, almost spilling out.

Each time we say goodbye, I'm tempted to tell her 'I love you', but I want to do it in person.

That will have to wait.

For exactly four weeks and three long days.

~

I'm lying in bed looking over our schedule for the next few weeks, wondering if I have any open windows where I could fly out to see Lily.

I'm getting desperate already.

I have a private jet ready to take me anywhere I want, but my schedule simply doesn't allow it. It would be easier without the time difference, but all the time lost—especially on the return flight—simply won't cut it.

I sigh, frustrated that I can't see her before she comes to visit me.

Four weeks left.

My phone rings, an incoming FaceTime call from the woman of every hour of every day.

"Hey, beautiful."

I've already talked to her on the phone and texted all day, but I'm glad to see her face as well.

"Hey, babe."

She's often out and about, wandering around campus or relaxing in a park when we have our calls.

Now, though, she seems to be in her dorm.

"I have a surprise for you," she says, a sly smile on her lips.

Then she moves the camera down her body, where she's wearing nothing but lingerie.

I groan out loud, feeling my cock swell at the sight of her.

As she's been out in public for most of our calls, we haven't done anything sexual over the phone; just the occasional sexting.

I didn't know if she would be up for it. It certainly is a first for me.

She seems more than ready for some action, spread out on her bed, looking like the goddess she is.

"Fuck, Lily. You look perfect," I tell her.

I get more comfortable on the bed, adjusting the pillows behind me as I lean back.

Then I move my hand down my body to my cock.

"Show me, Sebastian."

She's a mind reader as well.

I push down my boxers and kick them off before bringing my phone down.

Then I show her my hand working my dick.

"Lily, I love the lingerie, but I need you naked," I tell her, feeling the pre-cum run down my shaft as I jerk.

She quickly discards the lingerie, leaving her as naked as me.

"What would you do if I was there?" she husks, her own hand toying with one of her boobs.

"I'd start with those tits. Give them some well-deserved attention," I tell her, Lily copying my orders as I tell her to pinch her nipples and knead.

Her breathing deepens as she toys with her tits, and I hang on to every blissful second of it.

"Such a good girl, doing the things I tell you to."

"Then I would get to that cunt. Lily, are you wet?" I ask her.

She moans out loud, her fingers reaching her pussy.

"Fuck, yes."

I grip my cock harder, watching her finger work her clit.

"I would fuck you so good, baby girl. Make sure you'd feel me for days after I'm done with you."

Watching her, hearing the noises she's making, urges me on as I race towards my own climax.

"Sebastian, I'm close."

I watch mesmerised as she comes, her legs shaking as I urge her on with my words.

"Fucking perfect."

Watching her sends me straight over the edge, shooting my cum up my stomach.

Lily watches me intently through the screen.

When our breathing calms, she starts giggling, a slight blush to her cheeks.

"Gosh, I never imagined I'd have sex over FaceTime, but I guess there's a first time for everything."

She's glowing in the dim light of her dorm, her smile content as she lies down on her pillow with her phone in front of her.

Kind of like we're facing each other in bed.

"I do enjoy doing as many firsts as possible with you," I tell her.

It might be my favourite thing ever.

Doing new things with her.

Experiencing things through her eyes.

"You'd never had phone sex before?"

She almost seems timid to ask her question, which is adorable.

"No. You're my first baby."

I'm tempted to add 'and last', but decide to keep it to myself.

Reminding myself that this is all kind of new, and I don't want to pressure her or make her feel like I'm the overbearing boyfriend.

"I love all our firsts," she says, and the word isn't lost on me.

Why didn't I just tell her before she left?

It feels like we're having the same conversation through our eyes, none of us wanting to say the big words over a screen the first time.

"Four weeks," I whisper, reminded of another time when we were holding on to our control before crossing that line.

My self-control slipped right from my hands, and it might just do that this time around as well.

"Four weeks."

~

"Should I push you down the stairs?" Dean asks, making me look up at him, a frown on my face.

"What?"

"If I push you down the stairs, you'll probably be injured and therefore could be out of practice. Then you can let us all out of the misery of your sour mood."

Fredrick chuckles beside Dean, obviously agreeing with the fucker.

Am I really that moody?

"Shut up. I'm not in a sour mood."

But my tone isn't exactly cheerful.

He might have a point, but resorting to injuring myself to go see Lily may be taking it a little far.

"On a serious note, Sebby, you should try to get some time off to see your girl. We can see you're struggling."

I don't think I've ever seen Dean this serious, which says a lot.

Shit.

Maybe I am struggling more than I realised.

I could try to talk to the coach and get a few days off.

It's been almost two weeks since she left, which means we are soon at the halfway mark.

It wouldn't be too bad to ask for some time off.

I've never asked for it before, and it must be possible for family emergencies.

Missing your girlfriend may not qualify as a family emergency, but he doesn't have to know that.

"Yeah, I think you're right. I'll look at our calendar for the millionth time and try to come up with something for the coach."

It's at least worth a try.

The worst thing he can say is no, but then I would have at least tried to end this misery.

"Do that, and if that doesn't work, we'll always have the stairs."

~

I've just gotten back from practice when my phone rings. I instantly feel lighter, hoping it will be my girl on the other end of the line.

I haven't talked to her today yet, so I look forward to hearing all about her adventures in the warmth.

When I fish out my phone, though, it's the wrong Hastings on the other end.

I feel bad for the disappointment I feel when I pick up the phone to a smiling Luke and Jessica on the other end.

"Hey, guys."

I try to force some enthusiasm into my voice.

"Gosh, he's just as bad," Jessica says, a look of concern overtaking her face.

"What do you mean?"

Luke and Jessica let out a sigh at the same time; they even breathe in synch now.

"We just talked to my dear sister, and she looked like she's just witnessed someone kicking a puppy," Luke says.

Every time I've talked to Lily, she seems like her usual self. Our longing for each other is definitely there, but I try to keep our chats light and fun.

I don't want to bring her mood down when she should be having a good time on her trip.

A sulking boyfriend won't do any good.

"I miss her a lot," I mumble.

"Why don't you just invite her back?" Jessica asks, her frustration shining through.

"I want her to do the things she loves, explore the world. Don't sit here and wait for me to get back from practice."

Jessica rolls her eyes and takes the phone from Luke's hands, ready to give me a lecture.

"How the hell you were the relationship expert whenever this idiot messed up? I have no clue, because seriously, Sebastian, you need to take a page out of your own book."

Jessica isn't wrong; I was the one helping Luke find some clarity when he faced struggles in his relationship with Jessica.

It's very different when you're the one experiencing the turmoil, though.

Now I understand his perspective of wanting to protect the other person, even if it hurts oneself.

"I promised myself I wouldn't tell you this, as I hoped you would figure this out yourself, but I guess I don't have a choice. Lily told me herself that she wanted to stay in London with you."

At my expression, Jessica gives me a soft smile and a nod, reassuring me that yes, I did hear her correctly.

She wanted to stay?

And I didn't even ask her.

God, I'm a fucking idiot.

"But her trip? And her plans?" I ask them, feeling at loss.

Looking back, I recall instances when she didn't seem eager to go back, but then she would put on her brightest smile and talk about jet skiing and tanning, which made me think she was looking forward to it.

"She was scared you might want to go back to your routine without her," Jessica says, making me feel like an even bigger asshole.

Hell, how could I make her feel that way?

After my chat with the boys, I've made a plan.

I found a gap in our calendar where I could take the trip, if the coach gives me one-and-a-half-days off.

The biggest problem is that we have a game.

He might not agree to that, but I have to at least try.

I've never missed a game and will probably be lectured about having my priorities straight.

Right now, though, the only priority in my mind is Lily and making sure she knows how I feel about her.

I'm grateful for Jessica telling me, even if I wished I had figured it out on my own.

Sometimes, you need a little push from your friends.

"Thanks, guys. I'll talk to my coach tomorrow and hopefully go get my girl," I tell them, a beaming smile taking over their faces.

"Sounds like a plan."

~

"This is very unusual for you, Bennet."

Coach is looking at me strangely—probably wondering where his dedicated player has gone.

I'm sitting in his office, and I've just requested time off to go see family.

I can tell he wants to dig more.

If he does, I'm planning on being honest.

I have to go see her.

"I know, coach. I don't plan on making this a habit. My plan is to actually bring this specific family back with me to London."

Saying it aloud feels good.

Ever since Jessica told me that Lily wanted to stay in London, even if I don't know how long she's envisioning, I've felt lighter.

Knowing I'll have her here with me.

Over the last two weeks, I've reflected a lot on the loneliness I've felt at times in London.

I've never really thought too much about it until Lily came along and brightened my world—quite literally.

Before her, my days were just full of routine. I've done that routine every day, without question or dwelling about how it made me feel.

Then she came along, and everything changed.

Suddenly, I was experiencing the city through her eyes, and my perspective changed.

Doing life alone, when you've had the opportunity to do it with someone else, just isn't the same.

"Is this the blonde you've had around?"

I'm not surprised he's noticed.

Lily has been at every game, sporting my jersey and calling my name.

She's also been with me to the stadium most days, watching in on our practices and working on her paper.

During the last weeks, she even talked to Fredrick and Ian, who had some questions about pressure and nerves they wanted to discuss with her.

I've told them great things about my sessions with her, and the pride swelled when they asked me if it was okay for them to speak with her as well.

"That's the one," I confirm.

He gets a thoughtful expression on his face, and I wonder if he has his own family at home.

It's never crossed my mind to ask.

Coach is a very private man, never sharing too much with us.

Now, though, I'm curious whether he has a family or if football is his sole focus in life.

"I'll let you go, Bennet. But so help me God, if you don't manage to bring her back with you, we'll have a problem. You've been shit these past few weeks."

Leave it to him to be blunt and tell me exactly how it is.

He's not wrong, though.

I've been playing worse.

My sleep is a mess with tossing and turning until I'm exhausted.

Harriet has kept me well-fed as always, but my breakfasts have gotten worse by the day, as I wake up without an appetite most mornings.

"I plan on it. Thank you. I appreciate this a lot."

I stand and grab his hand in a handshake.

"Go get your girl, Bennet."

Chapter 32

Lily

I'm lying on the sun bed and pick up my phone for what feels like the millionth time.

Still no messages.

I've sent Sebastian several texts, and he usually answers right away, or whenever he's done with practice.

Today, though, it's been radio silent.

I've tried calling him, but I was sent straight to voicemail, which means his phone must have been off.

I even called Luke to ask if he's heard anything, but he just told me that sometimes the coach springs a twenty-four-hour challenge on his team, where they won't have their phones and will be solely focused on football.

Sounds rather extreme if you ask me, but what do I know?

He didn't have anything like that when I was there, but Luke told me it's only done once a year to shake things up a bit.

Still, I feel antsy not having talked to him since yesterday.

"You'll have no nails left soon if you keep that up," Mira says beside me.

I hadn't even noticed I'm biting my nails; my anxiety is through the roof. I should be relaxing, enjoying the beautiful day as the sun shines down on us.

Instead, I'm a nervous wreck, worried about not hearing from my boyfriend for a few hours.

"Shit, I might have to go and buy myself a drink. Maybe the alcohol would soothe my nerves."

"Sure you don't want a Coke Zero instead?"

I must be hallucinating, because that voice sounds just like the man in my heart.

I quickly whip my head around, and right there, Sebastian is standing, wearing khaki shorts and an open shirt, looking like any other tourist on this island.

He's here!

I jump up and run straight into his arms, finally feeling my nerves settling down, only to start right back up as my heart beats in my chest.

I hug him tight, breathing him in as his arms circle around me.

I lean back, looking into his eyes as he smiles down at me.

"You're here," I say, not quite believing my own words.

I wasn't supposed to see him until over two weeks, which felt like way too long.

"I'm here," he says before pressing his lips to mine and making everything feel right again.

This is right where I want to be.

In his arms.

When we break apart, Sebastian looks down at Mira, who's observing our exchange with a smile on her face.

She's been teasing me about being a love-sick puppy ever since I got back.

"Nice to meet you, Mira. And thanks for the help."

Help?

She knew about this?

"You knew about this?" I ask her, disbelief in my voice.

"Yeah, your man needed some help locating our hotel—wanted to surprise you."

Christ, I love him so much.

Knowing he's gone out of his way to make this happen.

How he's even pulled it off is something I plan to figure out, but for right now, I'm just soaking up the feeling of being back in his arms.

Mira gets up and takes off for a swim, leaving us alone.

Kait and Wendy are off to the spa for massages.

Sebastian looks down at me, softly pressing his lips against my forehead.

"I forgot to tell you something, back in London."

I feel my heart pounding in my chest.

The number of times I've regretted not telling him how I felt before I left England is countless.

Even more so, I didn't tell him that I wanted to stay.

If these weeks apart weren't enough, the clarity has never been this obvious as he stands in front of me.

"I love you, Lily."

He presses his lips to mine before I have the chance to say it back, which we can't have.

I end our kiss quickly, pressing my hands into his chest and my forehead against his.

"I love you too."

His smile is breathtaking, and as our lips melt together again, we chuckle when our teeth clash—neither of us able to contain our grins, which makes kissing a little more difficult.

It's perfect.

~

Turns out, all the girls knew about Sebastian coming here. Mira has never been the best at keeping secrets, but I guess the most important one to not tell was me.

We're all out in the water, enjoying a swim, and I'm grateful for my friends' support and approval of having a man on our trip.

Even though I've tried my best to put on a smile during our trip, they've seen firsthand how much I've missed him.

"So, Sebastian. How did you two meet?"

This should be fun.

Kait and Wendy still don't know our history together; they probably think I went to London and fell for the handsome footballer.

"We met when we were little. I'm her brother's best friend."

The girls let out a sigh, always up for a romantic story.

Sebastian looks up at me. I'm wrapped around his body, my legs behind his back, with his arms around me as he holds me against him.

"Fell in love with her somewhere along the way, and now we're here," he says, mostly to me, his look of tenderness matching my own.

I can't pinpoint the exact moment I fell for this man. It happened gradually and suddenly, all at once.

I've always been drawn to him, his character, and warmth toward the people around him.

His playful and flirtatious side is an added bonus.

The girls keep asking Sebastian questions, and I'm grateful to see them all get along so well.

We're in the middle of a discussion about our evening plans when I feel Sebastian's fingers moving dangerously closer to my cunt.

He can't be serious.

We're in the middle of the water, my freaking friends around us.

I look down at him, and he solely looks at me with a smirk on his lips before lifting a single eyebrow.

I'm experiencing a wave of déjà vu as he slowly moves his hand inside my bikini bottoms.

The last time we did this, the dark of the club, the noise of the music, and all the people around us masked the noises I was making.

Now we're in broad daylight, and even if no one can see his hand beneath the water, I'll have to stay quieter than I've ever been.

When he pushes his finger inside me, whilst continuing his conversation with the girls like nothing is happening, I nearly lose it.

It feels so good to be with him again.

And even though I'd love for us to have some privacy, I've also always loved our adventurous side.

We've had some great FaceTime sex over the last couple of weeks, but nothing compares to having his hands on me.

I stay as still as I can, letting Sebastian find the perfect rhythm as he adds a second finger to the mix.

"We should check out one of the restaurants on the dock," Kait says, and Sebastian curls a finger inside me.

I grip his shoulder tightly, struggling to control my movements and sounds, but hanging on to him as he continues pleasuring me.

"Yeah, Lily loves trying new restaurants, so that would be nice."

Just as he finishes his sentence, he circles my clit with his thumb, and I bite my lip to stifle the sounds wanting to escape.

Just as I think I'll either have to stop him or simply come undone in front of my friends, I'm saved by a group of guys riding their jet skis fairly close to us.

The girls turn around, watching them, and as the noise intensifies, so does Sebastian's movements.

"Come on, baby. Give me your pleasure," he rasps in my ear, sending me over the edge.

I lean into his throat, biting down as I come, not being able to hold back the moan escaping me.

Luckily, the jet skis seem to drown out my sounds to anyone else besides Sebastian.

"Fuck, I've missed you," he says, kissing me.

I hum against his lips, feeling drunk from his touch. "I've missed you as well—and your fingers."

I wink at him, making him chuckle.

~

We're lying in bed, Sebastian running his hands down my sides after the best wakeup call I've ever had.

Yesterday, I wanted to stay in and let him ravish me for the whole night, but he insisted that we hang out with my friends, telling me that he didn't want me to compromise my time with them even if he's here.

He told me he'd reward me afterward, which he did.

There hasn't been much sleep, both of us desperate for one another after the time spent apart.

"How would you feel about coming back with me—or coming after your trip—and staying in London?"

He's going back tomorrow, and I've been wanting to bring it up, but honestly have been too caught up in him to even think about anything else than being in the present.

"I'd love to, Sebastian. I never wanted to leave in the first place."

He grabs my hand, kissing my palm before he tells me about his battle of wanting me to stay, but also not wanting to stay in the way of my dreams.

Is it possible to fall in love with a man a second time?

Neither of us wanted to be the one to burst our bubble before I left, but it's clear that both of us have been struggling with the distance.

The first week wasn't too bad, as I was busy with meetings, catching up with the girls, and my family.

Whenever I had a moment to breath though, the longing returned and hit me hard.

I've grown to love my life in London.

Where Sebastian thought my wanderlust was all about travelling to different places, I've realised it was more about finding the place where I felt like I belonged.

I found that in London.

"Besides, we still haven't checked off the Harry Potter experience on your list."

"Yeah, then the list will be complete," I say, leaning in to kiss his chest.

"I'll make another list—make sure you can't leave me again."

Sebastian pulls me on top of him, my body draped over his as a blanket.

"Sounds perfect."

~

For the first time ever since I left London, I feel at peace again.

Then, the emotion starts building as I realise the changes to Sebastian's apartment since the last time I was here.

My favourite chair from my own apartment downstairs is now sitting in the corner of his living room.

All the small souvenirs I've picked up over the weeks are scattered on his bookshelf.

The kettle I've used to make my tea, along with my basket of different varieties, is sitting on the kitchen counter.

Before I left, he told me he'd keep the apartment and not to worry about leaving anything behind, as it could be in the apartment until I came back.

Now, I'm realising he's bought it all up here.

I feel the tears prickling at the back of my eyes, my hand going to my mouth as I take it all in.

"You okay, babe?" Sebastian has concern written all over his face as he comes over, soothing his hands down my own.

"Yeah, just my stuff."

I sniffle whilst he dries away the tears as they escape.

"Is it too much? I've terminated the lease, but if you want your own place again, I'll make it happen."

Gosh, this man.

He's everything.

"No, Sebastian. It's perfect. I was just surprised," I tell him.

"Okay, then. I've put away all your things and clothes, but you can just rearrange whatever you want."

There is a slight knock on the door, and Sebastian has a fond smile on his face as he tells me to go get it.

I squint my eyes at him, wondering what he's up to.

When I open the door, I'm greeted by the biggest bouquet of red and white roses I've seen and a delivery guy who is barely visible underneath it.

"Delivery for Lily Hastings."

I grab the flowers as best I can and set them on the counter as Sebastian closes the door.

I look down at the beautiful bouquet of flowers, Sebastian coming up behind me and resting his head in the crook of my neck.

"There is a card," he tells me, and I start roaming around carefully to find it.

I find a small folded paper and look to Sebastian, who shrugs his shoulders before gesturing for me to open it.

London isn't the same without you. Will you move in with me?

- *Sebastian*

"Like permanently?" I ask him, my excitement overflowing.

"Like permanently," he confirms, his own grin matching my own.

"I'd love that," I tell him, pressing my lips hard against his.

I turn around in his arms, and he grabs a hold of my ass before setting me on top of the counter, careful not to push over the flowers.

"Harriet will be here soon."

This day just keeps on getting better.

I've missed her almost as much as Sebastian.

"Perfect," I murmur, running my tongue along his bottom lip before biting gently.

"Yeah, everything is now."

Chapter 33

Sebastian

I've just finished a workout at the arena when the coach comes over.

I've been back for a few days but haven't been able to talk to him and thank him for letting me have a few days off.

"Got your girl, Bennet?" he asks, making me smile.

He genuinely seems interested in this; he might be a romantic after all.

"Yeah, she's actually up in the offices working on her paper. Thank you again for letting me have a few days off."

As soon as we got back, everything went back to normal. The best kind of normal.

Waking up together, Lily making breakfast before driving to the arena together.

I'll run by her as often as I can, or she'll swing by in the stands when she wants some air.

Coach asks me about the paper, and I tell him about her degree in sports psychology.

When she finishes her studies, she's not sure what she'll do next, but we'll figure it out together.

I'm sure she'll do great in whatever she decides.

"I'm glad to have you back in shape—got me worried there for a second. Make sure you keep her happy."

Relationship advice from the coach himself.

I really must have been in worse shape than I realised.

Maybe that's why he let me go in the first place.

No one wants a player who performs badly, and let's face it; as soon as she left, I was down bad.

"Got it, Coach."

We say our goodbyes before I hunt down Lily.

It's time to go home.

I find her in her favourite spot: over by the windows overlooking the field.

I stand there, looking at her as she looks down in her notebook, a thoughtful look on her face.

She senses my stare, lifting her head before a smile breaks out.

"Hey, beautiful."

I stroll over to her, and although I was planning on surprising her when we got back home, I simply can't wait.

I pull out the tickets from my back pocket and hand them to her.

When she realises what she's holding, she beams at me before she throws herself into my arms.

"Oh my God! I'm so excited!"

We're finally going to do the Harry Potter experience tomorrow, which she's been wanting to do ever since she got here.

I may have rented out parts of the park, not wanting it to be too long lines and lots of waiting, but she won't know that.

There will still be other people there; just fewer than normal.

This is partly why it's taken me some time to arrange it.

I wanted it to be perfect for her. Therefore, I had to pull some strings to make it happen.

~

"We have to get some souvenirs!" Lily exclaims, pulling me over to a shop where you can buy all things Harry Potter.

Wands, capes, owls, books: anything you would like from the universe of Harry Potter.

She browses the many rows, with me following her and putting anything she spends more than five seconds looking at into the basket I'm carrying.

The shelves back at our place are getting rather full of souvenirs, but I'll buy some new ones if we run out of space.

My girl loves her souvenirs which means they'll get their place in our home.

I may not have read all the books as she has, but we've watched every movie, cuddled up on the couch which have made the experience more fun for me as well.

Now, I get most of the references around the park, and the excitement bubbling over for Lily has been amazing.

All day, she's been glowing and having the best time exploring the sights. There have been rides, castles, and performances all around the park, and we've enjoyed every minute of it, our hands interlinked and hearts full.

~

We're out shopping for a gift for Harriet and her husband, who are soon going away on their trip.

They decided to go to Paris to reminisce about old times and the time they spent there. I believe that city holds a special place in their relationship, just as London always will be unique for Lily and me.

The city where it all came together perfectly.

We wanted to get them something, which turned into a shopping spree and bags hanging off my arms.

We've wandered into a jewellery shop, and when Lily goes over to a section with rings, I make sure to study her reactions closely.

I think back to the beginning of our time together in London and how we flirted about what kind of ring she would want.

Now, I'm eager to find out for real, but I don't want to make it obvious what I'm planning.

If I were to ask her what kind of ring she would want, she'd know straightaway, which is why I must be discreet in my observations.

Hopefully, I'll get it right.

She's gazing at a beautiful, elegant ring with a green gemstone as the centrepiece. The stone is sharp with clean facets that reflect the light. The emerald colour is a vivid, rich green that I know would look amazing on her finger.

Several smaller stones decorate the rose gold band, and I could already see how this ring would be possible to pair with a wedding ring.

It may not look like the most traditional silver engagement ring, but I know in my core that this is the one.

A ring that is perfect for Lily and one she would cherish deeply.

She lets out a small breath, almost unnoticeable, but it's there, and it's all the confirmation I need.

I'm definitely coming back here and buying this ring later.

Chapter 34

Lily

I've just finished a talk with Fredrick when Sebastian comes into the office I've been able to use at the arena.

Since I moved to London, we've kept up our talks about sports psychology, and during a game night at our apartment, the other boys asked me if it would be okay for them to talk with me about some stuff too.

I was a little stunned, as I'm nowhere near being a sports psychologist yet, which requires several more years and a master's degree under my belt, which I made clear to the guys.

Nevertheless, they've seen how it's been good for Sebastian, and they wanted to try for themselves.

For me, it's been a mix of fright and excitement as I've talked with them. It's been similar to my interviews with Sebastian, which I used for my final paper in college.

A paper that was rewarded with an A.

Talking with the guys on his team has given me lots of practical experience in the field, which ultimately was what I wanted after finishing my studies.

I never imagined I would be able to have that here in London, but everything worked out perfectly.

The team has even loaned me an office for my meetings, overlooking the field.

Sebastian comes over to me, and I link my arms around his neck, pressing my lips to his.

"I've missed you," I murmur. It's just been a couple of hours since I last saw him, but I'm finding myself thinking about him most of my day.

I've been eager to get back home, knowing I have a surprise waiting for him.

His whole family is back in the apartment, ready to watch the game tonight, which will determine if they make it to the Champions League final.

They were here just a week ago, so Sebastian has no idea that they're back to support him.

"I've missed you, too. Jealous that Fredrick got to spend more time with you than me today."

I roll my eyes at him.

He's got nothing to be jealous about.

He's the only man for me, and the one I spend most of my time with.

We make our way out of the stadium and over to his car.

Going home together may be my favourite time of day.

After the Ashley incident, she thankfully didn't make an appearance again. Sebastian has been talking about buying a new place, but I'm kind of loving our home right where it is.

That apartment holds so many memories.

It's filled with us and so many of our first.

And as we make our way up, the excitement builds inside me as we near the surprise awaiting us on the other side of the door.

Sebastian, being the gentleman he is, gestures for me to go inside first, but I'm quick to step aside so his family will be right in front of him.

"Surprise!"

The utter shock on his face when he realises they're here is everything.

Family is important to him, and I know he's had times here in London when he's been lonely.

Therefore, this feels like a small gift to a man who deserves everything and more.

We exchange hugs, his mom and I giggling as we talk about actually being able to surprise him for once.

He's usually the one with all the tricks up his sleeve, so it's good to be able to give him something back.

When his family goes to sit down at the dinner table, Sebastian holds me back, dragging me into his arms before kissing me breathless.

"Thank you, baby."

A day, a week, a month, or a year with this man, and I know he'll always get my heart racing as in this moment.

~

The final whistle blows, and I swing my arms around Sebastian's mom, who's crying just like me.

He did it.

They did it.

They are going to be playing the Champions League final.

The pride swells in my chest as I take in the atmosphere of the arena.

Fans are cheering loudly, hugging those around them, and celebrating as if they were the ones out on the field scoring the goals.

I may have been in these stands for the last seven months, but the fans around me have probably been here for years, cheering on their team and the dream of making it this far.

A monumental moment in this club's history, which they will remember for a long time.

I'm sure pictures from this game will be hung around the stadium like the other important moments that grace the walls.

When Sebastian comes running over, he talks with the security guard by the fence and gestures to me.

Then he signals for me to come down, and they help me over the barricades.

"Congratulations, baby! You did it!" I throw my arms around his neck, and he wraps his arms around the small of my back.

The back which is sporting his name, of course.

Ever since that first game, I've worn his jersey.

"I almost can't believe it," he says, dazed.

I certainly can.

His team has been on fire this season.

I'm far from a football expert, but even I can say that his team has been marvellous.

Hungry.

Passionate.

Driven.

And now, they'll be ready to take on the biggest stage of all.

At least for club football.

I kiss him, hard and quick, as photographers are lurking around, eager to get the best shots to print for their papers tomorrow.

They eventually found out my identity, and even though the online comments weren't all positive, it's calmed down.

I guess that's expected when you date a famous football player.

I would do it all over again for the man in front of me.

Chapter 35

Sebastian

"All ready?" Joseph asks me from the couch.

I'm getting ready to leave for the most important game of my career: the Champions League final, which is taking place tonight.

My whole family is here, together with Luke and Jessica.

"Ready as I can be."

The last few months have prepared my team and me for this match. We've played games, perfected our play, and worked for this specific moment in our careers.

Tonight, we can accomplish the biggest goal of our careers.

I feel ready.

The nerves that first started appearing when Lily attended my games have quickly become a sensation I welcome.

Together with her, I've worked on my mental game, using nerves to regain focus and adrenaline to perform better.

She's also been working with some of the other guys, who were like me.

They didn't necessarily feel they needed to talk with a professional, but as they got to know her and saw the progress I, Fredrick, and Ian had made, they approached me.

She's started her own freelance service where players can book appointments with her to discuss stress, nerves, sleep, and injuries in a comfortable setting.

Her spirit tends to draw people in, make them feel safe in her presence, which is less daunting than speaking to a strict professional.

Our team has a team of physical and mental coaches, but I do know some of us have struggled with connecting with them.

Opening up about your fears, goals, and aspirations can be scary. Talking with Lily has been a great path for several of us—taking the edge off.

With Lily, they meet a professional and a friend.

Or girlfriend for me, which I'm planning on changing soon enough.

If her brother allows it.

I'm experiencing a sense of déjà vu, knowing what I'm going to ask him this weekend.

The last time I had this kind of conversation with him, I told him I liked his sister.

A lot.

Now, I'm going to ask him if he's alright with me proposing to her.

It might be a little old-fashioned, and the correct way would be to ask their father.

To me, it feels natural to ask Luke.

It feels like a full-circle moment in our relationship, having his blessing to make us family.

Lily comes out of the bathroom, and I smile as I take her in.

I'll never get tired of seeing her in my jersey and having my name across her back.

Hopefully, it will be her legal name soon enough.

She walks into my arms, hugging me tightly and wishing me luck, even if I don't need it.

Her confidence in me is all I need.

With her by my side, I know I can accomplish anything I set my mind to.

I bring my lips to hers, enjoying the glide of her tongue against my own.

Joseph mutters something about getting a room, but I don't care.

He still insists on staying here whenever he comes to visit, which means he'll have to accept the PDA.

I'm not going to tone it down in our own home, and having a good make-out session has become the perfect pre-game ritual.

"Go get that championship."

~

The final whistle blows, and our team gathers in a big circle before we start jumping around, celebrating our win.

We fucking did it.

Dean grabs me in a hug, and I wrap my arms around him.

"We are the fucking champions!" he yells out loud.

Just as he says it, the anthem comes out over the speakers, and Dean looks like he thinks he has God-given abilities.

I shake my head at him, chuckling as our team belts out the lyrics together.

When the song ends, I make my way to the section of the stands where my family and friends are seated.

My mom, dad, and Joseph are the first ones I see. Lily, Luke, and Jessica are also here, together with Harriet and her husband.

I hug my mom first, tears running down her cheeks as she hugs me tightly and tells me how proud she is.

Next up is my father, who looks just as emotional, but he's able to keep the tears at bay.

At least for now.

When Joseph comes next, I'm looking over his shoulder for Lily.

Don't get me wrong—I love my family.

But I'd really like to greet my girl.

The one who's been here for most of the season and experienced every high and low together with me.

Supporting me and cheering for us, wearing my name across her back.

Finally, I spot her as she makes her way to me, together with Luke and Jessica by her side.

She starts running towards me, and I step away from Joseph, who looks a little confused, until he spots Lily and understanding dawns.

"You did it! Congratulations, babe," Lily exclaims as she jumps into my arms.

I swing her around before pressing my lips to hers.

"Thanks, babe," I murmur, the noise around us fading to the background.

Part of me still can't believe I actually got her.

After years of pining and wanting.

I may have won one of the biggest tournaments with my team, but having Lily in my arms feels like the icing on the biggest cake.

Her wearing my jersey? Another thing I'll never tire of.

Luke clears his throat beside us, but when I look over, he's looking at us fondly.

Together with his own girl.

"Got any love for your best friend as well, Bennet?"

"I got plenty for all the Hastings siblings."

~

I'm out for lunch with Luke whilst Lily and Jessica are off to do some shopping.

When we've ordered, I feel the nerves rising as I know what I'll ask of him—as soon as I find the words.

The last few days have been like a dream come true. Our team winning the cup after years of hardship and dedication to this sport that gathers millions across the world.

Having my girlfriend, family, and friends in the stands, cheering me on and celebrating our win made it all even better.

Nothing would be possible without their support along the way.

Especially Lily, who's been there every step of the way.

"I have something to ask you," I start, taking a deep breath and reminding myself that Luke is a good guy.

There is no reason for me to be nervous about this, but I guess my body doesn't get the memo as I sit there in front of him, my palms sweaty and heart hammering.

It's a weird feeling of déjà vu, a lot like our conversation months back, when I told him about my feelings for Lily.

"Would you be okay with me proposing to Lily?"

There it is.

Out in the world.

Saying it out loud feels daunting as hell, but I've thought about this—planned it for months—so the thought isn't foreign.

I haven't talked with anyone about it, though. Afraid Lily would find out.

She likes being sneaky, which is why I've had to keep this under wraps.

Luke looks at me with shock in his eyes, a dazed expression crossing his face.

Then it seems to really register, and he gets up to give me a hug.

"Fucking hell, we'll be brothers for real now. Of course I'm okay with that."

I hug him back, grateful for his blessing and support as I take this next step.

When we're all hugged out, we sit down again, and Luke is back to looking dazed.

"You're proposing before me. You just love to beat me, don't you?" Luke says, chuckling as we think back to the one time I beat him in go-karting.

"You planning on popping the question soon?"

Luke gets a fond smile on his face.

"Yes, I have the ring and everything. Going to do it when we're in Bahrain."

The city where they first met.

My best friend is a romantic, but I'm not one to judge.

I got my own plan for the proposal.

"Christ, when did we get so grown up?" I say, making us both chuckle.

We enjoy our lunch and when the girls catch up to us, I share a secret smile with my best friend, knowing what they have in store soon.

Epilogue

One month later

Lily

"Bennet, you really need to work on that stamina," I call to Sebastian as I climb the last remaining steps of the cathedral.

Since I moved to London permanently, we've taken this trip countless times. Sebastian has gotten accustomed to it, usually following close behind me.

Now, though, he's further back than usual.

I gaze out over the railing, taking in the sight of London in a beautiful sunset.

I'll never tire of this view.

I still find it just as beautiful as the first time we climbed these steps.

But where the hell is my man?

He's never this slow anymore.

I turn around, ready to call out to him, when I stop in my tracks, my hands flying up to my mouth as I take in the sight in front of me.

Sebastian, down on one knee, looking more nervous than I've ever seen him.

Holding out a box with a ring, I'm not able to look at it just yet, in awe of the man in front of me and what he's about to do.

"Oh my God," I whisper.

My heart is pounding hard in my chest.

"Lily Hastings. From the moment I first saw the name Bennet on your back, I've wanted to make that our reality. Will you do me the honour of marrying me?"

Cue the tears.

And not the cute ones.

Nope, I'm full-on crying as I nod my head, saying yes to Sebastian as he gets up before he slips the ring onto my finger.

I hiccup as I look at it and realise just how well this man knows me.

I remember seeing this ring—freaking dreaming about it.

From the moment I saw it, I knew it was what I wanted someday.

I didn't want to say that to Sebastian, though, not knowing if he even wanted marriage.

And especially not this fast.

I've never been happier to be proven wrong as I gaze up at him.

He gently takes hold of my face before pressing his lips softly to mine.

"The ring," I murmur against his lips between kisses. Sebastian winks at me, a proud smile on his lips.

"Yeah. I know my girl."

I'm gazing down at my hand, the ring catching the light and glittering in the evening sun.

This Cathedral just turned even more special to me.

"Lily Bennet has a rather nice ring to it."

"Sounds perfect."

Epilogue Two

Four months later

Sebastian

I'm sitting at the dinner table, together with my own family, as well as the Hastings.

I guess we're all kind of a family now. We've always been a family, but now, it's legal as I look down at the rings on Lily's hand.

I grab her hand in mine, running my fingers gently across hers as she smiles at me.

Mrs. Bennet.

I couldn't wait long enough to have that settled, and we had a small, intimate wedding with our close family.

It was the perfect day for my perfect girl and the start of our forever.

We're planning a bigger ceremony next year, where we'll have a big party and celebration.

We didn't want to wait years to get married, but we also didn't want to rush the planning, so we decided to have two weddings.

As I gaze over the rings, I catch Lily looking at me again.

We sat at this same table, around a-year-and-a-half ago when I first volunteered for her to do her project on me.

Little did I know, we'd be sitting here, married and happier than I've ever been before.

"Mine." I mouth at her, which makes her smile.

"Yours."

THE END

Closing words

If you made it here, thank you from the bottom of my heart for reading The Match. If you enjoyed the story, a rating or review would mean a lot.

Curious about the rest of the Championship Romance series?

Book 1 – The Race

Luke Hastings and Jessica Edwards

Book 2 – The Game

Alexander McGregor and Sarah Parker

Book 3 – The Match

Sebastian Bennet and Lily Hastings

Book 4 – The Break

Peter Centimo and Molly May Wilder

www.ingramcontent.com/pod-product-compliance
Lightning Source LLC
La Vergne TN
LVHW041109080826
845145LV00007B/1745
9788269483604